The Sentimentalists

Johanna Skibsrud is the author of two poetry collections, *Late Nights With Wild Cowboys*, which was shortlisted for the Gerald Lampert Award, and *I Do Not Think that I Could Love a Human Being*. Originally from Meadowville, Nova Scotia, Skibsrud lives in Montreal. *The Sentimentalists*, which won the 2010 Scotiabank Giller Prize, is her first novel.

ALSO BY JOHANNA SKIBSRUD

Praise for *The Sentimentalists*

'Johanna Skibsrud's remarkable debut is a novel at once lyrical and frank, the resonantly layered portrait of a man, a family and a place that will stay with you long after you read the last page.'

Claire Messud

'A probing exploration — now subtle, oblique, now forensic, scalpel-sharp — of the ramifications of a person's experience through the lives and relationships of those he loves. Of the way in which what we do, and witness, echoes through our lives, and the next generation's.'

Tim Pears

'It was with no small surge of recognition that I read Johanna Skibsrud's deeply moving *The Sentimentalists*. A brief, subtly written story of a grown daughter's investigation into her father's Vietnam war memories . . . It reminded me of Per Petterson's extraordinary novel *Out Stealing Horses*, both in its careful tone concealing harrowing depths of feeling and its exploration of the mystery that is one's father. *The Sentimentalists* was the surprise winner of last year's Giller prize, the Canadian Booker, and it's easy to see why. As an objective reader, I was engrossed by the elegant plotting and intelligent writing, by the questing after a truth that would never be found. As the adult son of a Vietnam veteran, I was, simply, moved to tears.'

Patrick Ness, *Guardian*

'*The Sentimentalists* deservedly gained wide recognition after winning the Giller prize. In rich, evocative prose reminiscent of Marilynne Robinson, Skibsrud knits together the history of Napoleon Haskell, a Vietnam war veteran whose health is deteriorating fast and whose memories are hidden behind a seemingly impenetrable wall . . . This is a story of quiet moments loaded with emotional resonance . . . It's fitting that a tale as complicated and absorbing as this eludes easy resolution.'

Observer

'With its themes of memory and remembrance, presence and absence, it is a beguiling story that lingers in the liminal spaces between what is said and unsaid . . . This is a slender novel, but its dimensions belie how much it packs in . . . Skibsrud, an acclaimed poet, shows her talent for elegant economy in her slow layering of mood. Densely rich, her novel demands concentrated reading, but the result is often haunting, plumbing both the unreliability of memory and its characters' inner states with emotional immediacy. With its ghosts, its keen awareness of surface tension, and its nimble dips below, *The Sentimentalists* succeeds in hinting at the truth of a person's life, located somewhere in between the visible and invisible.'

Sunday Times

'Johanna Skibsrud's first novel was the surprise winner of 2010's Scotiabank Giller Prize, often nicknamed the Canadian Booker. It is easy to see what impressed the judges. *The Sentimentalists* is a writer's book: lyrical, thoughtful . . . An account of the fog of old age and the fog of war, this is a moving testament to the fragility of the stories we tell about ourselves.'

Financial Times

'An outstanding novel born of the horror of Vietnam . . . The poet Johanna Skibsrud's subtle yet candid first novel, which last year deservedly won the Giller Prize, Canada's major literary award, confronts the aftermath of a Vietnam veteran's experience and its impact on his wife and two daughters . . . Skibsrud is a calm writer, and her prose is detailed . . . the emotional power is relentless. A sense of longing courses through the narrative, yet the irony of the title is well served; this is an intelligent, reserved novel, and is all the more moving for the restrained dignity that conveys not only the regrets but also the anger . . . Skibsrud is superb at evoking memory, the way random flashbacks dart into the mind and entire scenes are recalled with the vividness of a photograph . . . The scenes in which she observes her father and his dead friend's father are brilliantly handled. There are flashes of perfection in this muted novel. There is also an ironic humour . . . A philosophical intensity often surfaces; this is a thoughtful novel, reflecting on many dark issues. Yet all the while Skibsrud is guiding the personal story towards a darker one: that of war . . . The US army did not leave Vietnam as heroes. This collective horror has inspired some outstanding novels; this is one of them . . . *The Sentimentalists* is an allusive, intelligent and solemn work that articulates one man's horror and the way it became a communal lamentation.'

Eileen Battersby, *Irish Times*

'Johanna Skibsrud is a Canadian poet and *The Sentimentalists* is her first novel. It has won a prize in Canada and comes festooned with praise from Claire Messud and Tim Pears, both very fine novelists themselves. Its first theme is memory and the disabling distortions of memory, its second an exploration of the relationship between the narrator and her father . . . This is done with considerable subtlety and adroitness as the narrative moves back and forward in time . . . One of the many impressive things about this novel is its density. By this I mean that the author has managed with considerable economy to fill in the background to her characters' lives while keeping their present and immediate thoughts, feelings, hopes and fears in the foreground. We are with them in the here and now, but always made aware of the there and then. The tone is sober, reflective, sometimes lyrical, always intelligently probing . . . Novels which invite such questions are not necessarily the most gripping . . . nevertheless they may be more worth writing – and of course reading – than others which skim with agreeable speed over the surface of things. This is just such a one, remarkably accomplished for a first novel, not likely to be quickly forgotten.'

Allan Massie, *Scotsman*

'If you liked Nicole Krauss's latest book *Great House*, chances are you'll get on with this award-winning debut from Canada . . . Skibsrud has the knack of bringing things into striking sharp focus where necessary and her dense, haunting novel impresses.'

Daily Mail

'[A] sparse, tightly atmospheric short novel from a poet who has made the leap to narrative prose with poise and no small amount of skill.'

Big Issue

'The Sentimentalists has many excellent attributes but the best may be the persistent proposal that one can never know anything, certainly in regard to relationships with those one loves . . . A novel with some élan . . . Skibsrud, brilliantly and with assurance, veers away from the neat ending.'

Sunday Herald

'Skibsrud's beautiful first novel is subtle, sharp and truthful.'

The Times

'Heart-stoppingly vivid . . . Affecting scenes of frightened young men at war.'

Scotland on Sunday

'A beautiful tribute to a father-daughter relationship.'

Globe and Mail

'The Sentimentalists charts the painful search by a dutiful daughter to learn – and more importantly, to learn to understand – the multi-layered truth which lies at the moral core of her dying father's life . . . The writing here is trip-wire taut as the exploration of guilt, family and duty unfolds.'

Giller Prize judges (Ali Smith, Claire Messud and Michael Enright)

The Sentimentalists

JOHANNA SKIBSRUD

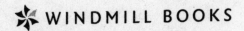

WINDMILL BOOKS

Published by Windmill Books 2012

2 4 6 8 10 9 7 5 3 1

First published in Canada in 2009 by
Gaspereau Press Limited Printers & Publishers

First published in Great Britain in 2011 by William Heinemann

Windmill Books
The Random House Group Limited
20 Vauxhall Bridge Road, London SW1V 2SA

Addresses for companies within The Random House Group Limited can be found at:
www.randomhouse.co.uk/offices.htm

The Random House Group Limited Reg. No. 954009

www.randomhouse.co.uk

A CIP catalogue record for this book
is available from the British Library

ISBN 9780099558361

The Random House Group Limited supports The Forest Stewardship Council
(FSC®), the leading international forest certification organisation. Our books
carrying the FSC label are printed on FSC® certified paper. FSC is the only forest
certification scheme endorsed by the leading environmental organisations,
including Greenpeace. Our paper procurement policy can be found at:
www.randomhouse.co.uk/environment

MIX
Paper from
responsible sources
FSC® C016897

Printed and bound by CPI Group (UK) Ltd, Croydon, CR0 4YY

For my mother

i sing of Olaf glad and big
whose warmest heart recoiled at war
E.E. CUMMINGS

Fargo

1 The house my father left behind in Fargo, North
Dakota, was never really a house at all. Always, instead,
it was an idea of itself. A carpenter's house. A work in
progress. So that even after we moved him north to
Casablanca, and his Fargo home was dragged away – the
lot sold to a family from Billings, Montana – my father
was always saddened and surprised if the place was
remembered irreverently, as if it had been a separate and
incidental thing; distinct from the rest of our lives. In this
way, he remained, until the end, a house carpenter. If only
in the way that he looked at things. As if all objects existed
in blueprint; in different stages of design or repair.

¶The Fargo place had been acquired by my father in the
first year of his sobriety, and by that time it had already
been pieced together from two and a half aluminum trailers and deposited in a lot – No. 16 – at the edge of a West
Fargo mobile-home park. To him, and therefore to us, it
was always his "palace" nevertheless, and he looked on the
additions and renovations that he made to the place over
the years of his residency there with particular pride.

The park itself was crowned by a large blue and white
water tower and the surrounding landscape of West Fargo
was so flat that my father could follow the tower, from
the other side of town, all the way home. He could drive
straight across the city on the carefully sectioned right
angles of highway, and it looked, as he approached the

3

park, as if the neat rows of long, low houses were, for the tower, a structural necessity. It also appeared that the park was in the tower's full shade. But, as he approached – as he passed the last four-way intersection and his own house came into view – the tower diminished, the houses lengthened, small front gardens appeared, and there was suddenly space for two or three cars in every drive. By the time he pulled into his own driveway, the water tower, although still large, was a peripheral structure six or seven blocks away.

¶The additions to the house had been made awkwardly before my father arrived, so that, from the side, the building appeared to be attached by several loose joints. Inside, the linked sections were marked by a step, and because the corridor was so narrow and long those steps were as much of a surprise to come across as a curve would be on a prairie-town street.

At the end of the corridor was the room my father referred to as the "second library" – the "first" having reached its limit years before. My father was a great reader and a great rememberer of things, though he never remembered anything in the right order, or entirely, and always had just little bits of all the books and poems he'd ever read floating around in his mind. The second library was the most lived-in room of the house and, besides the shelves of books that gave to it its name, it stored the computer, the TV, the exercise bike, and the photographs, in piles.

The photographs had been mostly those sent, over the years, by my mother and grandmother, and I knew them all well because they were the same ones kept in albums at my mother's house. They were of my sister Helen and me: posed for yearly school portraits, or else with our feet up on soccer balls.

Our early years were documented well in my father's house. There were shots of backyard camping, of our first dog, a golden lab named Roger, as well as stacks and stacks of Christmas concert photos, in which it is nearly impossible to identify a single subject.

A gap of four years in the progression of the photographs left most of our adolescence unaccounted for, so that, in going through the piles on my first visit to my father's house, at the age of twenty-two, I was surprised to find us – toward the end of the collection – suddenly grown. The documentation resumed itself only in sheets of uncut wallet-sized graduation photographs, and then in the newer, less dusty images of my niece, Sophia, which Helen had sent from Tennessee.

The second library was the designated smoking room when I visited. My father retired there after meals, and at half-hour intervals throughout the day. I avoided the room and tried to keep the rest of the house aired out as best I could. Sometimes, though, I would get it into my head that, like my father, I couldn't breathe – and then I would run back and forth along the corridor and swing the front and back doors quickly in and out.

¶In my father's last winter in Fargo, too out of breath to continue repairs on the palace, he became interested in the stock market. He upgraded his computer and after that spent nearly all of his time in the second library, rarely venturing into the long corridor that led to the rest of the many-roomed house.

He had set up the computer on a low desk next to the television, so that it was possible for him to watch them both at once, and he kept up on the progress of his few shares throughout the day, even watching them while he logged his obligatory mile on the exercise bike, which he had moved in front of the screen. When the markets closed in the evenings and on holidays he missed them and paced the room, he said, "like a bear."

¶The computer was part of a package deal that he paid for so slowly that the interest soon turned out to be double the cost. "I'm even getting a burner thrown in," my father told me over the phone in January, "and a fax machine."

"Doesn't all this depress you a little?" my sister Helen said a month later when my father's operations were in full swing.

"Dad," I said, "what in the hell are you going to fax?"

He didn't hear.

"I might as well," he told me. "At this price I can't afford not to."

By the third week of my father's career he had lost a total of $150 which he pointed out to us was pretty decent for a newbie.

"This is much safer than blackjack," he told me when he tallied the results and let me know.

"This might be the wrong economic moment, Dad," I said, "to get into this sort of thing."

"You may be right," my father admitted, "you may be right."

But my next communication from him was an e-mail he sent to both Helen and me, and it looked as though he had no intention of pulling out. It read, "Keep your fingers crossed and we'll be retiring to the original Me-hee-ko in very short order." Another message followed this one closely. "I've given up on the miners, but – doing a little research, and, third time being the charm, our next venture's going to put us in the running, my sweethearts. Hope you're feeling as lucky as I am."

Helen wasn't feeling lucky at all. "We've got to get him out of there," she said. "Henry will never put up with this shit."

¶Henry's place, tucked into the tiny town of Casablanca, Ontario – just twenty miles from the border of New York – was the site of all our childhood summers, and what all of us, including my father, secretly thought of as home. Still, when Helen first suggested that my father move there permanently to be looked after by Susan, Henry's part-time nurse for as long as we had known him, my father clung resolutely to the independent refuge of his palace, which he returned to every year, like a bird. But that next spring, after the stock-market winter, we moved my father, despite his protests, permanently to Casablanca. The palace was sold, according to Helen's direction, shortly before his departure, and it was arranged that my father's medical files be transferred to the North Country Veterans Clinic in Massena, New York, from where Susan – now fully employed – could drive his medication across the border, without delay.

¶It's a tall, upright building, Henry's house. Constructed on government money to replace the old family home – one of twelve original houses lost when the dam came through in 1959. Even now, Casablanca is a small town, but before the dam it was not even, properly, a town at all. It was only referred to by its intersecting county roads, and because of this was never officially recorded as being "lost." It wasn't until the dam came through that people started calling the place Casablanca. Like in the Bogart film, they had begun to "wait for their release" from a town that – never having fully existed – had already begun to disappear. But then, even after the relocation was complete, the name stuck – coming to refer to the new community of government-built houses that got strung along the lake road.

¶Although many of the original homes were, like Henry's, submerged, and others were burned to the ground, some had been simply lifted from their foundations and carried the short distance into the new town. Even the year before, with the construction of the St. Lawrence seaway, it was anticipated that the older houses could be so cleanly removed that residents were encouraged to leave everything in place inside them. For the most part, this advice went unheeded. People packed their belongings into boxes anyway, placing them in relative safety, in the corners of the rooms. But there were those who, curious to test the claim, left candlesticks on narrow ledges in the halls, books balanced upright on countertops, chipped teacups on high kitchen shelves.

8

One resident who left two mayonnaise jars balanced one on top of the other in the middle of her living-room floor, found them – upon re-entering her house fifty-two hours later and at a distance of several miles – upright still, as though they themselves were the axis upon which everything else had turned, seemingly less bewildered by their journey than she herself had been.

¶Henry's old place still lies buried some miles from his front door at the end of the disappearing road, which begins on one side of a small island and empties out into the water again on the other.

The dock at the end of the government house drive points like a long finger in the same direction; at the end of the dock, Henry's old boat is tied.

The remains of the rest of the original town (if that is what it can be properly called) can sometimes still be seen below the lake road, which runs from the town limit to an archipelago of islands in the middle of the large created lake: sections of fence posts, a crumpled church steeple, and pieces of the old foundations, which are marked at the water's extremity by long poles that stick out at odd angles around the edge of the lake – a warning for the boats that go racing by sometimes with their motors down, too fast.

2 My parents hadn't split yet when we first drove north to Casablanca to visit Henry, and we all lived together in the house that my father had built. It was a tiny place, tucked into the back of the woodlot we owned, just outside the small, Southern Maine paper-mill town of Mexico.

That house had also been a work in progress; a three-room cabin, clad in tar paper. Its inner workings – a network of exposed water pipes and electric wires – were always bare on the inside walls. Its front steps were missing, too; we'd always just gone in around the back.

The progress of the house was stopped entirely in the spring before I was born, when my father began work on *The Petrel*, a wooden boat built for my mother. It was a project that marked for him a spring of such passionate and uninterrupted enthusiasm, that, by the time I was born, he was hardly coming home at all. He slept, more often, curled up next to the boat in Roddy Stewart's old shed in town, and it was because of this that on the afternoon of my birth my mother drove herself to the hospital, my sister Helen in tow.

¶If, in the summer that followed, my mother complained – that she had been abandoned by my father, left all alone in the world, with two small children and a half-finished house – my father would reply with a wink and a wave, and in one small gesture describe to her perfectly the curve of the bow, or the slant of an imaginary sail.

If, when my father spent what my mother later claimed was their literal last-dime, in order for the *actual* sails to be sent (they were shipped, in mid-December of 1981, all the way from Delaware), my mother complained that they had eaten nothing but celery for a week, my father would remind her once again of the contoured coasts of Maine and Nova Scotia – from Booth Bay Harbour to St. John's.

The plans for my father's boat had also been sent away

for, and I remember that – years later, in a renaissance evening – the blueprints would be spread around our kitchen as my father consulted them, promising once again that we'd be sailing by spring. But, as I hovered to watch, and my father made fantastic, undecipherable scratchings with his carpenter's pencil on the page, I began to believe that the blueprints of *The Petrel* (where the constellations of lines and images had been drawn in the finest of ink, and on the thinnest of paper, which I thought hardly intended for human hands) depicted vast and astonishing kingdoms that were voyageable to him alone.

¶My father himself was not a water man – so when, in the summer of her abandonment, he was able to comfort my mother with the articulate gesture of an imaginary sail, it was because it was my mother and not my father who loved the sea. If it had been up to her, we would not have settled inland, but on the great and open Maine coast instead, the waters of which she had known as a child, having spent her vacations there, and which – even in my own earliest memories of it – remained still largely untouched and wild. It had become fixed in her mind. A blueprint for all of her future happinesses, which she could still, on those occasions, name.

It had been, after all, within those brief sea holidays that her own father had woken from his year-long nap to become, again, a human being – orchestrating great sea hunts in which the entire family scoured the tidal pools for clams. In which they speared fish, and tied white chickens onto lines in order to catch the blue crabs, which flocked like flies to the bait. And so it was the ocean that, for my mother, became the great elemental figure that was either missing, or to some degree at hand, when she searched in later years to solve the problem of her own and my father's lives. I think now of what a shame it was that the joy we, her own children, later found at the lake with Henry and my father was something that excluded her, and that she passed on her own love of the water only through the stories she would sometimes tell. Stories that made her seem, instead of closer, only further away – as though she surrendered herself, in the telling of them, to her own, separate, antediluvian underworld, which was what (influenced, I suppose, by the submerged town of Henry's backyard) we imagined all stories to be.

¶In the loneliness of the summer of my birth, when my father slept in town, my mother experienced on occasion pangs of such sudden and unexplainable grief that she would often drive us all the way into town to tell my father, in a resigned undertone, so as not to upset us, that she was dying – so sure was she that her grief had become a physical affliction, that it had begun directly attacking her heart.

This was another complaint that my father could always allay. He would smooth out her hair over her temple and forehead, and kiss her in the particular place that he had designated, behind her ear, for the specific communication of his love – which he sometimes found hard to say out loud – and tell her, in no uncertain terms, that very soon they would sail together in *The Petrel* of the white sails, paid for by a month of celery. My mother would apologize, her heart appeased. She would run her hand over her face and, with a little laugh (which served to establish the event in the already distant past), say, "I hardly know what came over me." By this route she returned to her more usual self, and she would pile us back into the car and drive home. Of the event she would make only a small note in the journal she kept in which to record our lives: *another episode today*, she would write. Followed by a record, as near as she could render, of the last thing that she had thought of or seen before the exquisite pain had begun. *Tomato plant. Obscure memory of Aunt Rose*.

In this way my mother attempted to uncover a pattern or a system to her grief, but there never did appear to be one, and the pain continued to erupt equally from the sight of an old photograph as from an untwinned sock. But after each entry my mother would go on to conclude: *it should not happen again*. And this conviction – that unhappiness, in herself and later in her children, should be staved off, then eliminated entirely – originated from that same source within her that assured her that the progress that my father was making on his boat, and that my mother was making on my father, and that my father's words were making on her heart, would be measurable and lasting things, upon which each of us could build.

¶Though my father remained with us for some time after that – scuttling the soft waves beside us during our growing-up years, our noble père petrel, floating just above the surface, as though held there by the last and most remote suspension of our faith – the boat, after that first summer, was also abandoned. My father working on it only in fits and starts, and, except for a single, brief renaissance which I have already described, this progress, too, ceased finally, long before I might have remembered it.

Still, the boat remained, perhaps especially for my mother, as though a physical memory; a last symbol of the one-time greatness of her expectations, and evidence that the future was still, in fact, in progress: that with the correct effort, tools and expertise it remained to be realized. Her optimism (having sprung from a deep well of unspeakable anger that at that time I could not guess at or understand), counteracted the effect of the years which had stretched the boat's boards nearly to bursting. It was as impermeable as the toughest and most enduring stain.

¶When my father finally disappeared from us in the summer I was twelve – after years of false starts, in which he spent his winters out west, returning to us later and later each year with the spring – the boat was moved, along with us, to my grandmother's house in Orono. In fact, my mother brought with us very little else; only what she could fit into the back of the car (a small Honda, about to embark on its final voyage). The rest of our things were doomed to remain, haunting the house that my father had built, living in its nether regions among the exposed wiring. At least, that is, until the land was sold to the paper company, and the house, eventually, torn down.

Really, there was no single or specific reason that we knew that that departure was to be my father's last – his exit at that time had been no different than on any other occasion – but I recall that we were very certain, and that even Helen and I, who were still very much children then, turned resolutely, when he was gone from the drive, back to the house. That we gathered our things deliberately in the large canvas bag that my mother had provided, and which, on more ordinary days, we had used for excursions to the beach or to town.

¶In the same way, I suppose, that for the drowning man there comes, though several times he raises himself above the surface, the irrefutable moment in which it is certain that he will not raise himself again, and the last bubbles of his final exhalations arise and disperse, and an invisible seal is drawn across the waves ... we gave him up.

Somehow, though, long after we had turned away, a phantom faith remained in me, long after its object had been lost. It came in bursts, in brief hallucinatory flashes, like the intermittent blinking of a dead satellite which still rouses itself on faulty wiring as though it were a dying star. So that even in those after-years, when my father had disappeared completely beyond the line of our horizon, it seemed as though, on fine days, I could see him still – a faint outline, a trace of himself – buoyed by the stubbornness of my memory, walking tentatively along the endless and otherwise uninhabited waters of my childhood.

3 My father had discovered Henry after an eight-year search that began the day my sister Helen was born. Because my mother had planned her family carefully (there were exactly two years between us and our birthdays were in the spring), Helen and I were eight and six

years old the summer my father drove us north to meet Henry. It seemed strange and it became a joke between the two men later, that it had taken my father eight years to track a man who lived – and whose family for generations beyond recall had lived – a four-hour drive away.

When we were young we called Henry our grandfather because we had no better term to describe the relationship. We did this for the benefit of other people, and never in front of him. "To stay with our granddad," we told the kids at school when we left at the beginning of every summer for Casablanca. At the government house, though, he was always just "Henry," and was not, in fact, related to our family at all.

In the small Maine town where we spent our early childhood, my father's having "come from away" (among other of his eccentricities) was enough to set us somewhat apart, so it was in contrast to this that we respected the fact that Henry had, on both sides of his family, lived in Casablanca, both the old and the new, for what was as good as forever. No one talked anyway of where they had first come from, and it seemed that it was enough to say that they were an original family from the original town.

¶On that first trip to visit Henry, my father packed us into the back of his red Datsun with a cooler that he'd filled with sandwiches and beer, and we all drove together, my father, my mother, Helen and I, all the way to Casablanca. He made it a point, when he could, to pass by on our way the towns we liked to pick out on the map, the ones with the foreign-sounding names. Oxford, Poland, Norway, Paris, East and West Peru.

When we got out in Egypt for gas, my father said, "These Mainers have the right idea. You can see the whole world without leaving the state."

¶My mother sat very still next to my father in the cab of the truck and every few minutes she turned angrily in her seat to rap three times on the glass. We knew what that meant. *Sit down. Don't fight. Be careful.*

Still it could not interrupt the perfect pleasure and excitement we felt then, bouncing around in the back of the truck on our way to a place we'd never been, with a foreign-sounding name more exotic than most.

"Isn't that the way of it," Henry would say later, when they lived together in the government house (to snap my father out of a funk and get him laughing). "It'll take a man most of a life to figure out that what he's looking for is four hours away."

¶In fits and starts my father's search for Henry Carey – father of the late Owen Carey – had been orchestrated in all the states of the union. He did not think to look in Canada. And though my father could recite with startling accuracy a description of the lake road, the dock, and the government house, long before he ever laid eyes on it; though he knew the inlets and coves where the remains of the old houses that could not be relocated were found, and could describe the lean of the semi-submerged steeple of the United Church with a borrowed gesture of his hand, he had no idea where it was, or if it in fact had ever existed at all.

"Pack some sandwiches then Henry," my father would

say, by way of a response, slapping his thigh and coughing out a laugh. "If it's that close, man," he'd say, "what are we waiting for?"

¶We stayed two weeks with Henry our first summer, and most of that time we spent out on the lake, fishing or otherwise just poking along the shore. Scrambling out onto the islands and imagining the original Casablanca that lay submerged below.

Dressed in bed sheets in Henry's backyard, we play-acted the lives of the former residents of the town, imagining them preserved down there – as if, like it was a ship, they'd gone down with it, and existed there still.

I didn't imagine then that Henry, who was alive and watched television in the evenings and fixed – hunkered down in his wheelchair – the motors on boats, had lived in that make-believe town.

I collected rocks that first summer along the shore, carried them in my pockets home to my mother, and laid them on the table as my offering because she never came with us in the boat. "This one is for how much I missed you," I said. "It's the largest one. This one," I said, "is for being happy, and this one is for being mad."

"Why were you so happy?"

"I got to steer the boat a bit."

"And why were you angry?"

"Helen wouldn't play. This one," I said, "is for feeling bad about how Henry always has to sit in a chair."

¶Owen had been a friend of my father's and then he was killed in the war.

We knew this only through my mother, because neither my father nor Henry ever spoke of Owen, and had perhaps forgotten (or so it seemed) the manner in which they were connected at all.

¶As to the linear details of the story, we knew only that much. Until I was a teenager, for example, I was under the impression that Owen had been a boyhood friend of my father's, and that my father himself had never fought in a war. These misunderstandings were not the fault of my mother, as she herself knew even less than we did, never having had the added intimacy of the long summer evenings and eternal, rainy afternoons in which we explored the peripheries of Owen's third-floor room. There, his collections of mica and rock crystal had been allowed to remain, as though through the centuries, lining the long windowsills and guarding the bookcases that housed adventure novels and instructional manuals for simple carpentry and windsurfing. These we thumbed through with the breathlessness of historians, absorbing the slightly damp smell of their thin pages through our fingers. When, from the sheer weakness of our wills, we took the mica from the shelf and – at the instant of contact – the dry leaves peeled and crumbled to dust, we placed it back as quickly as we could, as though we had been burned, and gazed in despair at our hands where the remnants of the rock remained, like a proof, on our skin.

¶After that first summer we spent all of our vacation months with Henry and my father. Even when he began going west for his winters, he still drove to meet us there.

First from Alberta, and then from British Columbia. They too were exciting and foreign-sounding names when they arrived on the return addresses of his occasional letters.

Sometimes, during the long school-year months that we spent with our mother, I dreamt of joining him there.

The first summer we left her alone, to make us feel better, my mother joked at how exotic our lives had become. "The children will be summering in Casablanca," she said in a fake English accent, and that night we ate off a tablecloth and she served us our juice in wineglasses, which we promised not to break. Then, when my father disappeared completely and my mother mentioned, not long after, our summering in town, our faces crumpled in a distress that was for my mother so familiar and sad that she quickly changed her mind. "No reason to interrupt our plans," she insisted, hurriedly, and that summer we went up to stay with Henry just as we had done before.

So for the four years that spanned the summers I was twelve through sixteen and we didn't hear anything from our father at all, we continued to spend at least half of every summer at the government house in Canada. Just Henry was there, and his nurse, Susan, who watched out for us too – but only part-time. I imagined that my father must have found himself in a foreign city too distant, finally, even to write, and I stopped, in those summers, entertaining thoughts of joining him there.

¶It turned out that what my father had found was Fargo, North Dakota. The year I was seventeen, his first sober year that anyone could remember, he resurfaced, telephoning my mother from that town. Shortly thereafter he resumed his summers at the government house, with Henry.

We kept up with the two of them mostly by mail after that, because both Helen and I had summer jobs by then or other excuses that kept us away. We didn't, after my father's return, spend much time at the lake at all.

It seemed, because of this, very sudden that my father grew old. It was Helen, finally, who noticed. She said, "He doesn't have anything keeping him there anyway. This year he might as well stay."

¶There really wasn't anything that tied my father to Fargo. It had been an accident in the first place that he'd ended up in the town. He hadn't, originally, even intended to pull over, for food or for gas, but by the time the palace was sold he had stayed fifteen years. In that length of time it was true he'd acquired many friends, but they were mostly old drinking buddies from the period of time at the beginning of his stay. When he got sober, those friendships dwindled, and by the time he left they had turned into a "checking up" on the guys now and then. He had his AA sponsor Gerry there – that was something – but they rarely saw each other either. "Don't need him like I did," my father told me. "I think the guy's in rougher shape than me."

And, of course, he had those two and a half welded-together trailers.

¶So in the end it seemed that my sister Helen was right, after all – as she often was, or assumed herself to be. My father loved the lake, and he loved Henry; they were, and had been for as long as I could remember, the best of friends. Even their brief political spats seemed between the two of them recreational and benign. Sometimes my father would even interrupt his own argument by saying, "I don't like disturbances in my place. You either lay off politics or get out." He would say this in his Humphrey Bogart voice. Our whole family could quote *Casablanca*, practically from beginning to end. We'd learned it as kids, after our first trip up to the lake with my mother and father. I think everyone in Casablanca knew that movie pretty well, but my father knew it better than anyone. He was best, too, at impressions. Especially of Bogart. He had a memory for that sort of thing.

It was Ingrid, though – "It's a crazy world … anything can happen" – that was his favourite. He'd put on his high Bergman voice when he said it, and sometimes just repeat it to himself, over and over. Like maybe Henry would have said, "Ye think this rain's gonna last all week?" And my father would wander around in his Bergman voice saying, "It's a crazy world …"

Other times he would look up at the sky if an airplane was overhead, or out the window, if a seaplane landed out on the lake, and say in another fake, falsettoed voice, "Perhaps tomorrow we'll be on that plane …"

He got a lot of mileage, anyway, out of that film.

4 So it was in the following April, after my father's last – stockmarket – winter in Fargo, that Helen left Sophia at our mother's house in Orono, and we flew

together to meet him out there. We rented a small U-haul trailer, and then the three of us – Helen, my father and I – crammed into the front of the old Datsun's tiny cab and drove the two days to Casablanca. My father smoked cigarettes out the window and Helen and I fought the whole way.

At first, Helen had forbidden my father to smoke in the truck, but then we were stopping every half-hour at rest stops and finally she gave in. "It's either that or spend another day on the road," she said. "Another hour would be unbearable."

Somehow, my father would always forget to open up the window when he first lit a cigarette, and it was the closest thing that Helen and I came to agreeing on the entire trip. After the first puff of smoke filled the car, we would yell out, in unison, "The window, *Dad!*"

It never failed, he forgot each time. We would watch him as he readied to smoke and every time felt sure that he would, just that once, remember. We found it unbelievable that he should forget *every single time*. But he did. It made us crazy in those moments. Watching him. Feeling the pressure build as we waited for him to strike the match – our cue to yell.

¶In reminder to myself that, although it felt like it might, there was no way that a two-day trip could last forever, I imagined the different ways I might recount its events even as they occurred. When my father, for example, shifted in his seat and Helen bumped into my hand on the stick as I drove, when he interrupted our long deliberate silences by saying, "Tell me stories, my sweethearts," I would

23

silently address an invisible, future audience: "He could never sit still," I told them. "He was always squirming around ... knocking us into the gearshift ... asking for stories ..."

When he spun the radio dial to the classic rock station and Helen spun it back after a song or two to NPR, saying, "Just for the news," I'd say, "and to make it worse, he and Helen fought over radio stations the whole fucking way."

¶Helen or I always got stuck in the middle when we drove, on account of my father's legs being so much longer than our own, and his smoking. We could never relax there, but sat straight as pins, our knees bent in toward the gearshift, cringing away from his spontaneous, unbearable hugs, and waiting for the relief of the yell that we shared every time he lit up a smoke.

¶It really did seem impossible that the trip would end. Cleanly, I mean, completely. The way we expect things to end when they do. When a story is told, and the past tense is used.

I can imagine, for example, that we're out there still: Wisconsin, maybe, or else cutting through the Upper Peninsula, passing Escanaba, skirting Lake Michigan, heading towards Sault Ste. Marie at the Canadian border. Driving that same red truck that is junked behind Henry's government house now. The truck I'd climbed as a kid and later, red and itchy from the fiberglass of the cap, scratched from my legs patches of prickly skin. "It wasn't all that long ago, you know," my father said often on that trip east, whenever we recounted snippets of this sort of memory to him. "You always make it sound as if it happened a long time ago." Then, a little later, to break a silence: "How does the time pass so goddamn quickly?"

¶On the one hand it's true. I can remember climbing onto my father's shoulders as if I were doing it still – balancing there, a leg on each side of his neck, my hands in his hair, then stepping off onto the roof of the cab. I remember how my foot felt leaving his shoulder, how the muscle beneath his light shirt sprang back into its place as my foot left and settled on the solid lid of the truck. I remember showing my pimply red legs to my mother, bits raw from my scratching, and her voice, irritated, saying, "I don't understand why he let you climb on that truck." There were little bits of glass, she told me, buried in my skin and that's why they were so itchy and sore.

On the other hand, it's hard to believe that those legs were my own. And neither is it easy for me to believe that the broad shoulders of that man, springing back to their shape underneath a light shirt, were the shoulders of my father.

"How does the time pass so goddamn quickly?" my father asked often, out loud. "I wasn't consulted," he said. "I can tell you that much. If I had been it wouldn't have happened so fast. You know how old you two would be if I was in charge?"

"How old."

"Eight. You'd both be eight," he said. "All kids should stay eight years old forever."

We'd just passed Escanaba and as we drove the light was on the window, a small and perfect globe, dipping up and down. Sometimes it was far and other times it was very close, nearly smashed on the glass. Insects, and even a small bird had already been caught that way, and this was evidenced by coloured smears on the windshield which were also reflected (in longer and darker flickering shadows) on the dash. The sun, however, was safe for many hours, until, so gradually we could not have pinpointed the moment, it simply disappeared.

"I miss my tower," my father told us a little later, as the Datsun strained its way up a steep slope. "I always knew exactly where I was in Fargo. Hills are nice, but they're not practical. How does anyone get home around here?"

"And also, you know what?" he continued, after a pause in which we heard only the gunned motor groan up the last rise of the hill, "I didn't know what I was missing until I wound up in Fargo. Yah, it's true," he said, mocking his adopted accent. "You betcha, kids. I drove this exact way with your mother thirty years ago and you'd think things would have changed but they haven't. I remember all of this exactly and nothing's changed at all. It's just I never noticed these goddamn hills before."

¶My father had been sober for twelve years by the time we arranged for the landfill department to drag his trailer away. Twelve years by the time we convinced him to sell his few stocks, pack his computer into the U-Haul, and move to Canada for good. Fifteen years since he'd been hauled downtown with a DUI as he sped through West Fargo and wound up staying there. Staying, so he said (even when he was free to go) because the roads were straight and because he didn't know a soul.

It had been seventeen years since my mother had called him from a Poland hotel with a billboard outside that said, "We Sell Sleep," and told him, "The war can't explain you forever, you know. I think you should be gone by the time we get home." Accordingly, then, my father had packed his belongings and headed west.

That was the first and only time that my mother had mentioned, to my father, the war.

¶When my father said, "Where did the time go, god-dammit?" I thought of it as if it was really a place that it got to. A place that looked a lot like the palace in Fargo, or the inside of my father's boat, which remains, now, the original image in my mind for the realization that time can somehow just slip away.

¶We got to the Canadian border early in the morning on the second day of driving. Even my father was a little worried by then. We knew that if we were suspected of our true intention – depositing my father in Casablanca, on the other side of the border, for good – we would certainly be denied entry. Instead, we had decided to say that our plan was to pass into Canada only briefly, in order to bypass the lake – but no one felt particularly certain that this was going to work. There was no one else in line when we arrived, so to make things worse, we had to linger suspiciously at some distance in order to review the offhandness with which we hoped we would reply, before finally creeping forward to the open window.

The official peered groggily in at us when we did

finally reach him, one heavy eyebrow raised. "Nothing to declare?" he asked, when my father said as much.

"Tell him something," Helen hissed suddenly, though this was not in the script. "They won't believe nothing."

"It's true," my father said again to the official, ignoring Helen. "We have nothing to declare. We're just going to be in your country for a couple of hours. It's just shorter this way. See?" He held the map up, but the official didn't glance down to where my father pointed, or in fact respond at all. "If they just made the roads straight around here," my father continued.

"Or if that lake wasn't in the way," I said.

"Don't joke with them," Helen hissed again, through her teeth.

There was a long pause and then the official suddenly scribbled something down on a page he had in front of him. He looked up at us again. "What's the relationship?" he said. It was a question we had not anticipated, and so for a moment did not properly understand. It was my father who clued in first, and when he did, he answered so quickly that he stumbled a little on the word.

"Father," he said. And we nodded our heads at the official in agreement. "I mean, I'm their father," my father said.

"Okay," the official said, seeming bored. "And what's all that?" He motioned behind us to where the back of the truck was piled high, and the U-Haul dragged.

"I'm moving," my father said. "This is all of my stuff. It's nothing much really – just regular things. Books."

"Mind if I take a look?"

"Sure," my father said, and he made to get out of the cab.

"No, you stay there," the official told him, and then got

heavily down from his booth and moved around to the back of the truck. He waved over a couple more men, who were just standing around, and they followed. We watched them when we could, straining our necks, through the rear-view mirror. "Nothing much," my father said. "I said: not fucking much."

"Shut up," said Helen.

"Nationality?" My father asked, in a deep fake voice. "Drunkard," he responded to himself, in his best Humphrey Bogart. "'A citizen of the world'. Do you think I should have said that?"

"Shut up," Helen said again.

¶"That's a nice computer," the official said, when he came back around. "I just got the same one for my oldest boy."

"Oh, it's great," my father said, once again loud and friendly. "And quite the deal too, wasn't it?"

"I'll tell you what," the official interrupted, as if he had a deal to cut with us as well. "I can let you on through, but I bet they give you a hassle coming back the other way."

"We'll only be gone for a couple of hours," my father said.

"And we're American citizens," added Helen. My father snorted through his nose. I think he was thinking about Bogart.

"Even so," the official said — he was apologetic now — "I'm just saying you might have a bit of a delay, with all of this stuff. It might end up being quicker just to turn around. Go back through customs here. I bet they don't hassle you so much if you haven't actually left the country."

He pointed behind him to where a road cut back to the short bridge that would return us to US customs.

"You mean just turn around here?" my father said. He looked around at Helen and me gleefully; I could tell that he was enjoying himself now. "Should we take the man's advice?"

Helen, pointedly, did not say a word. "This is silly," I said quickly, giving my father a look. "Let's just give it a try."

"Well, decide pretty quick," the official said. By that time there was a lineup behind us.

"Alright," my father said, and hit the gas a little hard.

¶We crossed the bridge in silence. "Well, fuck," my father said on the other side. We switched spots and I drove, which pushed Helen into the middle. "This is already the longest day of my life," she said, buckling herself in, "and it's only eight o' clock."

Then I felt her go stiff beside me. My father was getting ready to light up a smoke. I tried to concentrate on the road but I couldn't help it, I saw it. Saw him slide the cigarette from his pack and stick it into the side of his mouth, saw him fish out a book of matches from his pocket, and saw one match ripped, the book folded, and him ready to strike.

We didn't say a word. We were still thinking "Maybe," and we held our breaths, waiting. As usual, it wasn't until the first smoke puffed its way into the cab of the truck that we yelled. At which point my father apologized and rolled down the window – just a crack – so that the smoke spiralled up, and got sucked from the cab in a tunnel of wind.

5 I don't have many pictures of those early visits to Casablanca. It was my mother, not my father, who took the photographs. But the few I do have evoke in me a sense of moments which were perfect – self-enclosed – and which inspire me to imagine, briefly, that I've been like that. Uninterrupted. Completely absorbed by things. I am certain, though, that as they first occurred to me I never did feel quite as anchored in those moments as I am now willing to suppose. Even with how much we loved the lake, I remember that in those early years, and even more so later on, we were often terrifically, nearly fantastically, bored. It was in order to idle away those long, seemingly endless afternoons that we created the backyard stories of the old town: that original Casablanca, which lay submerged three or four hundred yards from Henry's kitchen door.

We must have known, and then ignored for lack of real evidence, that Henry, and a few others we saw regularly around the lake, could still remember the original town. That they perhaps even felt it was to the old rather than to the new that they more fully belonged. But because they hardly spoke of it, they did not interrupt our dreaming, and perhaps were even instrumental in leading me, at that age, to the false presumption that a thing could, quite simply, be forgot.

¶While Helen and I had still been making arrangements to fly out and bring my father east, he called one morning to tell me that he'd received, from Helen, a digital image of my niece Sophia and myself. It had been taken several months before when Helen and her husband had stopped to see me in New York on their way north to ski at Stowe. That had been January. It was cold everywhere. Stowe was so cold that Helen had spent most of her time there cleaning up spilled hot chocolate in the lodge with Sophia. New York was cold, but, "Don't think you're special," Helen said when she came through. "It's cold in Tennessee too, you know."

My father, however, had the real temperatures. After he told me about the photograph and praised his new printer ("It's just regular paper I got in there," he said, "but it came out looking pretty high definition"), he told me that the thermometer had been hovering at negative thirty for four days and that he hadn't had water for a week.

"What do you do?" I wanted to know.

"I've been melting snow," he told me. "It's not as though there isn't enough of the stuff, goddammit."

He'd been buying his drinking water, like always, he said, and melting the snow from his porch to do his dishes and to fill the toilet tank.

"But I can't piss in the toilet anymore," he said. "It stinks too bad."

"Where do you piss?" I asked, and pictured him shuffling out onto the porch in a forty-below night, his piss freezing above him in an arc. But: "I just go into a milk jug," he said.

"Can't you get someone to come out and fix your pipes?" I asked. "I mean, have you talked to someone about this?"

"Who?" my father asked me, "who would I talk to? It's my pipe."

I told him that someone would certainly come to look at his pipe if he called, but he said, "Oh, well, I had Lloyd over to look at it with me a while ago. It's just that the heating tape's all rubbed off, that's the problem."

"Well, I hope it fixes itself then, Dad," I said.

"Me too," said my father. Then, to change the subject, he said: "Gold's up."

"Oh, good."

"Not too good," he warned. "We don't have any gold. I'm into medical devices. This one company – they're just waiting for the FDA to approve and then they're going to just about own the market with this new pacemaker. Everyone needs one. They also do catheters and that sort of thing. Oh and AIDS research – I've got a few shares in that."

"AIDS research?" I said. "You can buy *shares* in that?"

"You can buy shares in everything," my father told me proudly. "Your uncle Clark told me about that one. He thinks it's big."

"Well, good luck," I said.

"Okay, I'll let you go. I just wanted to tell you about that picture, though," my father said. "It's really special, you know, Honey. I've got it sitting out here in the kitchen so I can look at it while I melt my snow."

"This is silly," I said. "Will you just call someone? It sounds like the third world over there."

"It is the third world," my father said. "But you should see my computer!"

He laughed for a while at his own joke, then asked, "Do you know how frickin' dirty snow is, though? It looks beautiful, alright … all white and pristine … but you should see all the crap that's in it."

33

"Get some more of that tape or something," I said.

¶There were two things I didn't know about my sister Helen on the drive east, and one of those things Helen didn't know either, and one of them she did.

The thing that she did know was that as we packed my father's belongings into the U-Haul and drove east, her husband Tom was packing his belongings into the back of his van to drive west. He had been offered a promotion, and the position was in Omaha. It was an offer he simply couldn't refuse. But Helen could, and by that time she already had. When we got back to my mother's place she said, "We'll be here just two or three more days. I want to head down as soon as I get 'the call'." She placed exaggerated emphasis on these last words, opening her eyes wide and bending at the knee as if pretending to brace herself against something invisible, which appeared to be quite large.

"What call?" I said. Sophia was paused halfway up my legs, giggling. Her feet were on my knees, and her body was arched out, away from me, so that her hair brushed the floor.

"Hi, Mom," she said.

"From Tom," Helen told me.

"From Daddy!"

"What?" I said.

"He's moving to Omaha," said Helen. "He'll call us when he's all moved out."

That was how Sophia and I learned about that.

¶The thing that neither of us knew was that she had carried with her, on that interminable drive east, a pearl-sized lump on her left ovary. It would be another four months before a routine check-up revealed it to her, and by that time it would be roughly the size of a pear. It was benign, the doctors said, but that didn't make a difference to Helen.

"Other people say they could feel something wrong," she said when she called to tell me, "you know, *inside* them. They say things like, *I just knew* ... stuff like that. But I didn't feel anything. I still don't."

¶It was late summer when Helen found the lump, and a few days after it was detected, she had it cleanly removed. After that, she was back to her usual self, and in fact, seemed more upbeat than she had in a while. Every week she called with a brand new plan for herself, and for Sophia. Meanwhile, they had moved up from Tennessee to live with my mother, and in the fall Sophia had started at the same school Helen and I had attended. My grandmother had been dead for three years by then, and my mother was grateful for the company.

¶In October, Helen had driven up with Sophia to visit my father and Henry at the government house, and reported that my father had settled in "relatively well." He had his computer set up in the bedroom, but his books were still in boxes. There was no second library, and not even a first, at the government house.

He did his crosswords on the porch by day, while Henry tinkered with the busted engines of boats. At night, he'd pick a book up at random from a box on the floor and read – from the middle, later to discard it without reading it through – as Henry worked out math problems which he designed himself in front of the television, sometimes reading his mysterious findings to my father out loud.

My father was happy, he said. As he always had been at the government house. But there was something missing in his voice when he said it, and he continued to refer to the palace with a nostalgic pride that seemed to convert it, in memory (always, with the resilient optimism of a house carpenter), into something different still.

He had again bought and maintained on his bedroom computer a few shares in one or two shifting stocks, but it appeared that his enthusiasm, regarding even this particular project, had waned. When, a little later, Helen discovered the extent of his credit-card debt and insisted that my father give up trading altogether, he – without too much of a fuss – did.

¶The following February, I made the trip up with Helen and Sophia. We stayed at a hotel in town, because Sophia was allergic to cigarettes, and visited with Henry and my father in the cold vestibule where the coats and boots were kept, talking a little anxiously about how Sophia was liking her new school, what sports she was into, and that sort of thing. Everyone, even my father, seemed – in the discomfort of the vestibule – overly polite.

Then Helen and Sophia and I went tobogganing on the small hill by the house while Henry and my father watched from inside. Intermittently, my father would come out on the porch and smoke a cigarette, and when he did he would shout things at us, giving a big hearty laugh and a cough, with whatever it was that he said. "Go get 'em, Honey!" he'd yell. Or, "That as fast as you can haul that thing?"

After that we went out to dinner at Geppetto's, a greasy Italian restaurant, one of the only food establishments in town. Again, my father spent a lot of time out on the porch with his cigarettes, even through the brief meal. He would peer in at us through the glass of the window while he smoked. Sometimes he'd wave, and when he did we'd wave back in an exaggerated way.

¶Later that winter, though, he would grow despondent. His health had worsened quickly since the move, and by mid-winter even moving from the kitchen to his bedroom on the other side of the hall had become a chore. He remembered his palace, that last bastion of progress, more frequently as the winter lagged. "Well, I've burned all my bridges now," he said to me one particularly bad night over the phone, and I felt then a sense of remorse so large – for something that I had not done and so did not know how to understand – rise sharply inside me with those words. It was as if I believed in that moment of my father's sorrow, as he himself seemed to believe sometimes, that Helen and I, who had been complicit in his final relocation to the government house, where he was destined now to die, were responsible, at least in part, for this eventuality.

The government house, which he had looked forward to every year – where it had seemed, in each ensuing summer, possible once again for him to become a new and different sort of human being – had become for my father his last and only option. "I'm gonna die in Casablanca," he sometimes rumbled in his Bogart voice. "It's a good spot for it."

When he said things like that, though – when he quoted Bogart – we knew he was in an optimistic mood.

Casablanca

The negatives that haunt our ideals ... must be themselves negated in the absolutely Real. This alone makes the universe solid. This is the resting deep. We live upon the stormy surface; but with this our anchor holds, for it grapples rocky bottom.

WILLIAM JAMES

1 But then, in the spring, after my father's first winter in the government house, I found that it was my own life that came, quite abruptly, to an end. It happened simply. While standing at the intersection of Dominion and Queen, on my way to work one day. In that briefest moment of repose, when the lights, lingering momentarily between red and green, had paused traffic in four directions. So that, even when I could hear again the cars lurch from their standing positions forward, even when I could feel again the thrombotic pressure of their blinking lights, now stalled, now pulsing with longing, to turn left, to turn right, I myself stood still, caught at that particular intersection from which I could go no further. The birds on the top strand of the telephone wires whose notes – on previous days – had remained only a background melody that I had not heard, seemed suddenly to hit precisely the chords which resonated in my own stopped heart. And though a great pressure continued to propel the earth forward, tilting it along its axis in a precise and singular direction as it went, careening through space, in another, I myself remained static and unmoving.

Finally, though, blown free at last, I floated up over the intersection and looked down at the great expanse of suburban streets below. From that perspective I was able to see all the way from King in the north to Woodburn – that great artery which led out to the highway. All the way from Halifax Street in the east, to Division in the west. And then farther, and yet farther – almost to the city limit, where the streets gave way, in brief consent, to stubborn grasslands; to the few surviving farms there, studded by the roadsides with gigantic billboards, which seemed to announce, in eloquent sentences, the beginnings and the ends of the earth.

I was by that time suspended at such a distance to myself that I was no longer aware of the traffic, the birds, or the patterns of objects which had arranged themselves into various systems below, and hovering at that furthest distance, my only thought was that I would like, very much, to go home. But home was by then so arbitrary, so vague a location, with no precise dimensions in space or in time, that it was by an unexplainable coincidence that I was then returned with a sudden jolt (the impact of which was comparably slight) to my own body. And that there, after adjusting my bearings, so that instead of heading east down Queen toward my place of work, to which I was never to return, I retraced my steps north, instead. That I followed the stream of light that broke, in sporadic and ever-changing patterns, along the centre of Dominion, all the way back to Brooklyn, from where, gathering what few belongings I still recognized to be my own, I made my way to Casablanca.

Perhaps all of this will seem slightly less surprising if I divulge at this point that the event I have just described occurred exactly ten days after stumbling upon the man who for six years I had been intending to marry as he made love to another woman. A woman who happened to look very much like me. On top of a stack of clean laundry, which, earlier that day, I myself had piled on the bed.

Although in the days that followed I would say next to nothing of the event, and would come to believe, as had been insisted, that what had occurred had in fact been the smallest of infidelities, and so particular in nature (having occurred in what was already now the past) that I might come to overlook it entirely, I could not seem to drive the image of that woman, who had resembled me so closely, from my mind. Nor forget the expression on her face, of surprise – and perhaps, vaguely, of recognition – as she put on my clothes, which she picked from the floor (her own having been lost, irreversibly, in a tangle of laundry and bed sheets) and walked out my door.

¶After altering my route, and tracing my steps back to Brooklyn that afternoon, I packed what little I could into two duffle bags, and left the man I had been intending to marry, as well as all of the accumulated objects of his existence, except for myself. Left them because, quite simply, they were his. And I, in my thirtieth year, who had accumulated what appeared to be next to nothing, took a taxi to the airport and flew to Canada, to live – on grounds that I could not reasonably articulate – with Henry and my father.

¶Overall, I would have to say that it had come as a disappointment to live within the particularities of a life; to find that the simple arithmetic of things – which I thought I had learned by rote, but was now unsure from whom, or what it was that had been learned at all – was not so simple. That it was not, in fact, combination alone that increased the territory of living in the world. And that love did not, of its own accord, increase with time. That it could find itself just as easily divided by things. And that there was nothing to do when it left you but bite your tongue and wait for its return. As though it was a small bird, which sometimes thought to wing itself across the city – but would, almost always, thinking better of it, arrive again in a rush, to the sill. Oh, I would have waited like a dog for seven lifetimes for that bird to appear, if I knew that it would continue to come! If I knew that it would continue to look in again with fondness at the small room, which it had thought to leave behind; at a life of knowing; of closeness, and foibles. Of regrets, misdeeds, and small, personal ecstasies.

The objects, just as they were – so delicately arranged for it there, all lined up on the shelf – would seem so precious to the little bird, then, that it would wish its heart was not so small, or nailed so closely to its chest.

¶But so often had I approached that window myself, with no concerted attempt at flight, that by the time of the incident at Dominion and Queen, I had become convinced that it was in fact an impassable divide. So that when, all of a sudden, and without my expecting it – though I had in fact been for many years teasing at a small crack in the glass with my mind – the window shattered, I almost did not recognize it. That the window had become a window again – paneless, glassless – an empty space from which I was required to depart. And all the world, in its variations, its illimitable pathways and directions, seemed then not terrifying as I had imagined that it might, but only very dull in comparison to the bright and tangible details of the room I was obliged to leave behind. After all, however ultimately far off from the rooms that I once had dreamed of inhabiting, the colours and textures of that room were at least visible, handleable, real, and therefore seemed more pleasing and worthwhile to me than an empty succession of shades of grey.

It is only from a distance that abstractions are, after all, desirable, or even possible. And none was desirable enough to me then to warrant an actual course of action, replete with telephone calls made to real human beings, and the inevitable initial chill of a new and as yet unlived-in life. So that, staring dully from the vantage point of the airport waiting room as I made my way to Casablanca, there seemed nothing that might satisfy me; no route that the sudden introduction of a window might illumine; no life that would not also contain the great sorrow which hung from me, then, as though it was a separate object. The one thing of any weight that I had, it seemed, so far acquired.

¶ "I just need a break," I told Helen when I called her from Henry's house two days later. I had put off calling until then because I didn't want to explain anything to anyone. Because there was in fact very little to say. I put it in its simplest terms: the other woman I had found, the flight from New York. But Helen was hardly ruffled by the news. "Good for you," she said. "But don't drive yourself crazy up there. Why don't you come home?"

Because I didn't know the answer to her question, I didn't say anything, and shortly afterwards I hung up the phone.

¶After putting the phone back in place on the government house wall, I gazed around Henry's kitchen, where for once I was alone. I was looking for something, I guess. Some object that might prove to me that the events of the past week and a half had been real. Some object that I could not have recreated or imagined for myself otherwise if, as seemed more likely then, I was only dreaming. If I had not actually returned to Casablanca, with only the contents of two duffle bags, neither of which – when I rifled through them in the mornings – seemed to contain anything at all.

But there it all was. The usual items of Henry's kitchen, as well as some things I'd forgotten, or never seen. A hanging plant by the porch door, which had recently been installed. The joke barometer which read, permanently, "wet and windy," which I hadn't noticed for years. The remains of a specific, unimaginable lunch on the stove.

¶I hardly spoke at all to Henry and my father in those first few days at the government house, and miraculously, when, for the first time I might have wanted him to, my father did not ask me for my story. Instead, I walked alone, back and forth along the lake road, hoping to uncover my old feeling for that place, which was something that I had also, perhaps, only forgotten. But whatever it was that the government house had at one time been to me seemed buried at such a remove that it might have been someone else's memory that I hoped in those moments to recall.

At night, I lay up in Owen's old bedroom, where I had slept so many nights as a child, and felt nothing at all, except for the static hum of electricity from the floors below. A sad and irreversible change had occurred, it seemed, and the great and open space which I had always felt within me, that I had thought, in fact, had been me, had disappeared so finally that I could not hope to resurrect it, or feel again that lightness at the exact centre of my heart as I had on so many occasions before. When, in that very room, I had harboured in me an expectation of a world so vast, and of such incomparable beauty, that I could feel it loosening the muscles of my throat; a disturbance I could hardly endure.

¶On those occasions, what I had feared most was only that the space I felt in me so palpably then might remain all my life in the unbearably empty state in which it had arrived. So to find that, on the contrary, it could disappear completely – and without a trace – without ever having been filled; that it could be compressed so soundly within a body that inside would remain only the mechanical procedures of the lungs and the heart, was a great surprise. But what was more of a surprise was to realize how many years had passed without my noticing its absence, and I wondered how many more years would have gone by; if the window had not smashed, that is. If my life had not reeled to halt on the corner of Dominion and Queen.

I had thought in those years, I suppose, having learned the lesson from my mother, that it was foolish to ask for too much out of life, afterwards only to live in the wake of that expectation, an irreducible disappointment. But what pain, I thought now, could be greater than to realize that even the practical reality for which you had assumed to settle upon, did not hold – that even that was illusory? Would it not be better, then, to set your sights on some more fantastic and rare dream from which even in failing you might take some comfort in having once aspired?

¶In the mornings I would remain as though asleep for as long as I could. I did not want to wake to find myself there, again, in Owen's room. And in those first moments, my eyes shut tight, I tried to imagine that I had not really arrived there at all. That it had been only a trick of the universe, which had, temporarily, sucked me back from my great, disembodied adventure over the suburbs of New York into that particular body, that particular room.

Hoping that this was the case, I would stay in bed sometimes for an hour or more before I rose, listening to my father and Henry beneath me: banging the breakfast dishes and shouting to each other across the hall in immense, pithecoid, monotones.

What, I wondered, were they hoping to communicate down there?

When I could wait no longer, I would rise and join them, lumbering heavily down the stairs. My father would greet me as I arrived. "How's my little wanderer?" he'd say, and I would grimace a reply as I wandered to the sink to rinse a mug and drink three cups of coffee by the window, while he sketched out the day's crossword puzzle, and Henry grunted through his perusal of the obituaries and the local news.

Unlike Helen, or my mother, who called several times a day to do so, my father and Henry did not ask me any questions, and my father was often jovial in the old familiar way, which I had missed over the course of his first winter at the lake when, even in the briefest of telephone calls, great silences had occurred. These my father blamed on the government house, whose emptiness in the winter, he said, gave him the creeps, and resulted, conversely, in a claustrophobia more severe than any that had resulted from the narrowest of his forsaken palace halls.

2 But then one night, hardly a week into my stay, as I lay unsleeping in Owen's room, I was interrupted from my own silences by my father's scream, which rose to meet me as though in a single spiral. It was a wail so loud, so long, and so inhuman, that I thought, at first, it was not my father's yell at all. That it had come instead from within me; the echo perhaps of a great loneliness which I was only then beginning to understand.

Or perhaps it was only the ghosts of the house, I thought, who, after so many years of fluttering in corners, of rearranging the dishes and books on the shelves, had thought to call out – weary of our disbelief – and make themselves known.

But, when the noise continued, now loud, now low, now muffled by curses, I realized that it was my father who yelled, and I flew down the two flights of stairs to the entrance of his room.

By then the noise had stopped, and for some reason I hesitated at my father's door.

"Dad?" I said. Cautiously. "Dad?" I entered, but did not find him there.

I met Henry in the kitchen, where he had wheeled himself, bleary eyed. "What's going on?" he said. Then a third yell was heard, a fainter and most human yell, which ended with a moan as I flung open the bathroom door, and located my father.

He was crumpled in a ball, slid somehow between the bath and the toilet bowl, his legs curled into his chest as he clung to one arm and swore through his teeth. "It's my fucking arm," he told me. I turned on the light and both of us flinched in the glare. My father's limbs were long and bare, and looked like the imaginary limbs of a large bird, as if drawn from the inside. I was afraid to touch him in case he broke into several pieces, as once, reaching to a high shelf in my grandmother's house, I had caused a glass animal to shatter. And in fact when I did bend toward him he yelled out at my touch. "Honey, Jesus!" he said, and I had to reposition myself so that I could reach his far side without jarring the hurt arm, which he held onto so tightly that the fingers of the hand that held it had gone white.

Henry was in the doorway. "Holy Mother of God, Napoleon," he said to my father, for the first time, in my memory, using his real name. We sat there for nearly half an hour on the bathroom floor, Henry in the doorway, before my father allowed me to help him dress and move to the kitchen, where we sat for another hour and a quarter, wondering what on earth we should do.

"We'll wait until the morning," my father said. "See what it looks like then." But already my father's shoulder was the bruised colour of an eggplant. "If I could fucking breathe," my father said, "it would be better." It was true, his breath was coming now in short bursts: harsher, and faster than normal.

Finally, I managed to help him out, in the pitch darkness, to Henry's car. We walked slowly, Henry shouting encouragement sometimes from the lit-up porch. But every time my father stepped onto his right foot, a pain shot through his side and into his lungs, taking root in his damaged shoulder, and what he took to be his heart, so that with each step he gave a short yell, almost a "Hup! Hup! Hup!" keeping time as we walked. And when at last he was tucked into the passenger's seat and I leaned in to fasten his seat belt as carefully as I could on his opposite side, he yelled out: "Jesus, Honey, are you TRYING TO KILL ME?"

I shut the door and got in across from him, and we drove the two hours to the border, crossing over at four-thirty in the morning, my father finally asleep, his face on the glass.

¶The shoulder, we were told, had been broken cleanly across the blade, at the exact point of impact when, having become disoriented in the night, my father had fallen against the bath thinking he had already traversed the small distance to his bed. By ten o'clock in the morning, however, we were already on our way back to the government house, my father's shoulder taped and in a sling. He stared out the window almost the whole way and seemed to not have much to say, nor care if I did, though I tried – my first concerted effort since I'd arrived – to make my voice light and unworried sounding as I made small remarks about the things, for example, that we passed on the road.

But then, just before we got to the border, for some

time by then returned to silence, my father said, "If you could remember one thing and have that be your life, what would it be?"

"What would it be for you?" I asked.

"I asked you," my father said. "It was a question for you."

I felt suddenly tired. The effort of conversation was after all a very great one, and this was more than I had bargained for.

"I don't know. That's a difficult question," I said. And we left it at that.

3 That first summer that my family spent at the lake with Henry, the summer I was six years old and Helen was eight, was the only summer my mother accompanied us. We spent the largest part of it on the water: in Henry's boat, or on the dock, or swimming near there.

Mostly, my mother stayed on shore.

Tellingly, what I remember best of all is the way my father and Henry were together. To me they seemed – even Henry in his chair – symbolic nearly of perfect health and joy. Henry, with his great arms that were big as the trunks of young trees. Who would let us climb them sometimes, leaning forward in his chair, and pressing his fists to the floor, so that Helen and I could take turns clambering up them and onto his back.

Sometimes, he would bellow out a laugh or a shout as we climbed, or lift out an arm when we were nearly to the top, in order to disrupt us, or otherwise fold us in, easily (our weight to him had little meaning) and tickle us, or hint at it, anyway, until we giggled, gasping, from his grasp.

My father, too, had once been a large man. In those first summers at the lake – especially then, as we were still so small – we called him Paul Bunyan, because he looked to us just like the giant statue of that imaginary man that we passed when we drove through Rumford, Maine.

He could carry both of us, jumbled on his back, and run with us from the dock so that for a moment we would be suspended all together: my sister, my father, and I, for a split second in the air.

Then there'd be the sudden hit of water and the tangle of our bodies. I, the weakest swimmer, would climb up, a little frantic like a kitten, to my father's neck and shoulders.

Or he would throw us – alone and high – away from him, and from the dock. He was so strong that we could really fly, and in those two or three seconds could even think, and remember, truly, how it felt to be like that: moving up and out, and away from the dock, from my father's arms. Anticipating the water, but not too much. Trying not to, anyway. Trying not to waste those moments. To stay in them as much and as long as possible.

¶In the evenings, my mother and father fought softly in their bedroom, retreating there when my mother, inevitably (each evening as I recall it) stood up, abruptly, from her chair and said, "Let's continue this inside."

Often I wouldn't notice there'd been an argument until I heard those words. I was, by that time, so accustomed to the way they spoke: bitterly, to one another.

Is it possible that I didn't really think of them at all?

Most of my memories of that summer are of Henry and my father. Of their bodies, of the lake. My mother, I remember differently. As though she inhabited a complete and separate world.

Eventually my father would bang out of the bedroom and return, jovially, to the porch from the continued conversation, with two beers. One for Henry, one for himself. And he and Henry would resume, happily, whatever conversation they'd been having.

What did they talk about so eagerly in those days?

¶Helen and I would be reading, or playing with the Lego blocks we'd brought along. We built an entire city that summer, in the corner of the porch as I recall. Sometimes, we would be out on the lawn, playing in the near dark, and from there we could hear only the rise and fall of my mother's voice, sharp and high. Then Henry and my father's voices would start rumbling in, the sound broken with their barks and shouts of laughter.

We would have to be called in, those nights, by my mother. But we played late. She would remain in her room for an hour or so after my father banged the door to leave her. But when she emerged again, she was always more total, more in love with us than she had been before, and she spoke to us so softly, and with so much tenderness, that we were afraid, nearly, for one another. We became, within her bursts of maternal caring, more fragile than we thought we were at other times.

We loved to feel that way again, come evening. Our bravado given over; laid aside. Our loud and brash behaviour of the day dissolved. And we didn't worry about her. No, we didn't think of her at all. She, who in those late evening hours, in the extreme of her comfort to us, must also have been attempting some comfort for herself. Our ability to return to her, to fall under her spell each evening, must have been, for her, a great relief.

¶Away at a week-long sleep-away camp for the first time late in August of that same summer, I experienced a home-sickness so acute that I can still remember the taste of it, cottony and sour on my tongue. Even then, it was Henry's place that I longed for.

I had received, I suppose – in those first two weeks we spent at the lake with Henry – such a distinct notion of what home was, or could be, that I have been unable, to this day, to give it up entirely. So that even now, when I have become aware of the complex system in which we were all, even at that time, involved (though we as children didn't know it), my longing for that home remains as strong as ever. The only difference being that the home is absent now. Perhaps it never existed at all – or at least not in the way I imagined. I long (I admit) for nothing, but admitting it changes very little and – even after everything that's happened since that first summer – there is some-thing in me that expects that I will find what I am looking for, still.

4 When we returned from the hospital, we found that Henry had opened all the windows and the kitchen door that led out to the porch, so that the air, still cold

though it was June, had located every corner of the government house. Any hint of the usual smell – the stale smoke and cats and grease, and another, partially sweet, partially antibiotic smell which I could never identify – was gone. It was very cold in that kitchen, but it did not smell.

I fixed a pot of coffee then picked up the half-finished crossword on the table and handed it to my father.

"You'll have to help me," he said, indicating his right arm.

Henry arrived, and inspected my father. "I thought they'd have you mummified by now," he said. I poured them both a coffee. My father balanced his in his left hand and sipped it awkwardly, as though he had never held a mug of coffee in his life.

He tossed me a pen, and pointed again at the crossword.

"Help me out," he said. "I'm stumped." Then he laughed uproariously.

¶That evening, after Henry gutted fish on the lawn, chucking the insides to the screaming cats, I fried the fillets with garlic and margarine, because there wasn't any butter. When the windows, in late afternoon, had been closed, the stale smell of the kitchen returned quickly, so that the scent of fresh garlic and fish cooking was a welcome change. They were perch. Big ones. And Henry had caught four. I cooked all of them – and so perfectly even Henry acknowledged it.

"Well, I taught her right, I guess," he said when he found that the flesh pulled, as we dug into them, cleanly away from the bone.

¶After the meal, we were quiet. My father smoked a cigarette or two, inclined slightly toward the window by the kitchen table, which he had opened. As he exhaled, he seemed to become emptier – as if he pushed the smoke from his body just a little too hard.

The light from the porch illuminated only a small oblong shape on the lawn directly outside the door, and everything else fell away into darkness. In the distance, however, the lights from the houses on the far end of the lake, as though answering to our own, lit up the water enough that we could make out along its edges the poles which rose from the buried foundations on that side of the lake like the long bodies of ghosts.

One time, years before, we had watched a documentary that some divers at a local scuba club had shot, with footage of the bottom of the lake, near where Henry's house had been. There were no images of the house itself, but Henry had clearly identified the old dock that he and Owen had fished off and jumped from on hot summer days. I reminded Henry of that film then, because it seemed to me suddenly strange that those murky images of the bottom of the lake existed in that moment just as they had at any other time, just not illuminated by a light – equally small, and equally fleeting – as the ones that lit up the opposite shore.

"Yep," Henry said, as though nearly swallowing the word. "It was still there, boy; I thought I would cry."

I had never in my life seen Henry cry, and even as he said it, he did not look like he might. But it was strange to think that the sadnesses of Henry's life had then, and at other times, too, necessarily existed among us – just without my noticing them, and I wished, fiercely, staring out at the dark lawn between the light of our own porch and the corresponding lights on the opposite shore, that I could return things somehow – to the way that they had been. That I could resurrect the old house. In substance, in fact. So that Henry and his family could live forever there and never now depart, in their various ways. And never now feel in their throats the catch that I detected then, for the first time, in Henry's. But what – and here was the dilemma, even in metaphor – would have happened then? I mean, to everything else? To my father, for example? Or to me?

When I tried to say something of all of this to Henry and my father, though, I only stumbled on the words, and finally interrupted myself to exclaim out loud, "I hardly know what it is that I'm saying at all!"

In fact, I felt I did know. It was something very particular that I wanted to say; it was just that I had no way to say it.

¶Henry remained quiet, and only cleared his throat loudly once or twice as my father and I continued to speak for some time after that, arguing a little, but to no purpose, interrupting ourselves and one another, back and forth. He stared, first at my father, then at me, and the same expression crossed his face then as on certain occasions of my childhood, when the pastimes of Helen or I (a half-built tree fort that we had constructed in the yard, a rope swing slung into shallow water, or, later, an announcement of an intention to go for a ride on Bonehead Henderson's ATV) provoked not so much a fear, but a general paternal apprehension — that it was the world that was dangerous and untrue and that we, in the face of it, were bound to be defeated, at least in small ways, because of it. At least lose the casual confidence with which we'd slung a rope over a low limb, or slid in behind the terrible Bonehead as he gunned the motor on his vehicle and took off as though into outer space.

So then, after some time had passed, and my father and I had wrapped our way around again to the beginning of our argument, Henry said, "Let me tell you a story."

Casablanca

1959

from them blue depths nor choppering down skies
does Dr Present vault unto his task.
Henry is weft on his own.
Pluck Dr Present. Let his grievous wives
thrall lie to livey toads. May his chains bask.
lower him, Capt Owen, into the sun.

JOHN BERRYMAN

1 When he was a very small boy the moves they made
dotted the pink of the map of the world, which was
Canada and the United States. Once, they dipped down
into the orange of Mexico, and he shoved his thumbtack
firmly there. Sometimes it was hard to do (his thumb
smarted) and sometimes it was easy, the wall soft. Into
the northern reaches of Alberta, and somewhere near the
border between the Carolinas. Until the back of the pin
touched the flat of the wall. Until no space showed there.
When they again relocated and the tack was removed,
there remained a small but permanent hole in the wall,
which he left behind. Also, and this he took with him,
there was the small dark point in the map where the page
had been pierced, so that when Henry looked at the map
of the world in Ontario, where finally they remained, he
saw not only where they were, clinging precariously to the
underside of the Canadian shield, but also where they were
no longer.

We're moving, Henry, his father would say. And, jostled
aware as if from attempted sleep, Henry moved, following his father's voice as though along a bouncing train
corridor.

¶When they returned to Ontario, his father too sick to
work, they lived again in the house of his earliest childhood, which Henry remembered as acutely as if it was he
who had been pierced through with it. As if it had caused

in him a deep but narrow hole – the shape of which corresponded directly to any mention of his grandfather's place, and contrasted sharply against the abstract geographical dimensions which had been previous homes.

¶The house was old and had plenty of ghosts, or so his grandfather said, and all of them were the ghosts of Henry's grandmother. Henry was taught to distinguish between them just as other boys are taught to distinguish between stones, or trees, or birds. He began to recognize them, as his grandfather and his father could do, to sense them as one after the other they came or went, busy with ordinary tasks. As they brushed by him, in and out of doors, reclined in the sitting room, or were found otherwise bent over the lawn where the garden used to be. One young as when his father was a boy. One shy, and always laughing. Another serious. One ill in the bed. Another hanging clothes on an absent line.

There was, his father told him, a ghost for every moment of a life, and some lingered, as the grandmother's did; making themselves, for their own, very private, reasons, known. One day, Henry's grandmother was at last sketched so precisely that Henry woke to find that he had begun to know her, not in the flickering stages that her ghosts described, but instead, at once – as herself – entire. When that happened, he realized that, like his father and grandfather, he had come to love her – perhaps more, or anyway more simply, than he loved the living members of that house.

¶By the time he was again asked to move (this time by the power company in the year the Seaway came through, the year that Owen was twelve), Henry had lived so long in his grandfather's house that he had forgotten that at one time he and his father had slipped from the map of the world like pins. And the thumbtack, which still pierced map and wall in what was now Owen's room, and which Owen observed nightly before drifting to sleep, had spread a chalky brown stain around itself, in a ring, obscuring not only the precise point where it pierced, but also all of Southern Ontario and most of New York.

¶Henry had married Jacqui in the summer after high school, and in early December, Owen had been born. They stayed with Henry's father at the old house and Henry worked at the mill in town, saving his money in a coffee can for the house they planned to build.

There was a spot for it already. In the clearing behind the old house, where, as a boy, Henry's father had often taken him, spreading his flat hand out in the direction of the far edge of the field and remarking, in a clear and unembellished phrase, the precise wording of which he never varied, that one day the land was to be Henry's own.

Over the remaining years of Henry's childhood, his father had kept the clearing trimmed of weeds and of the spruce that every spring returned, often reminding Henry of his efforts there, and thereby also of the field's existence. When Henry visited the place on his own, even in later years when his father ceased to mention it, he would feel a sudden chill run through him, as though his father were again laying that heavy hand on his shoulder, and sending that unmistakable coldness up and down his spine.

Once they were married, Henry was eager to build Jacqui a house of her own there, but this had not been what his father had intended. He had wanted, instead, for the land to spring up in corn. In sweet beets, or cherries. In a way of life that would not, that is, be the life of the mines, which had turned his own lungs too black to work. Or of the mills, or of the factories, where men – Henry's father said – equally and oppositely turned pale.

Factory work was not real work, Henry's father said when Henry got a job in town.

But there were many things, Henry thought, that his father didn't know or understand. For example, there were things that you had to be born to. That it took more than to point across a field and say something out loud. More than six acres of cleared land. Also, Henry had promised Jacqui something. He wanted it too, and perhaps even more badly than she. To have a life of their own. One that would not be riddled with the confusion of the various and unpredictable departures and arrivals of his grandmother – or of his father for that matter, who had begun to blow through the house sometimes as though he too were a ghost.

¶But when Owen was three, the mill closed down, and the money that Henry had saved inside the coffee can began to disappear far more quickly than it had risen there. He got a job fixing up houses in town, but it bothered him more than the factory work had. Some days it was like he and Jacqui were doing nothing but rattle around, like they were their own last two dimes knocking into one another at the bottom of a can.

Then, in the year after the mill closed – Owen had been four – and after a short convalescence in which every day she insisted she was stronger – Jacqui died.

Henry drove his father's Chevy into the brick wall of the closed up mill in town and wound up in the hospital with a fractured spine.

¶And so it was because Henry himself did not speak of the house that he would have built, or of Jacqui again, that it was Owen's grandfather who told him of his mother, painting her picture alongside his own wife's ghost, so that the two women came to live for Owen side by side. It was startling the way that things could, in the end, come to exist like that, within the same small space, when they had seemed in life to need, necessarily, to exist for themselves alone.

This is what Henry thought when he began to overhear his father describe Jacqui to Owen, in this or that particular way (Jacqui wringing clothes out in the sink as though strangling a goose, or bending with a shout, to hide her hand of whist from Henry with the wandering eye), and he regretted bitterly in those moments that he had not had the chance to build Jacqui a house of her own, where she could have lived – instead of in parts – as a whole. Entire. In the way that she had been for him in the first instant that he saw her – in the sixth grade, which he had had to repeat – as she stepped into the room, and he had felt it enter him in a single rush. That first – absolutely whole, absolutely perfect – moment of human love.

¶It was Henry who broke the news to the grandfather, and to Owen. Over breakfast the next day, having waited a full twenty-four hours after first hearing the news himself. Having made several telephone calls to the newspaper and to the fire department, to verify that, indeed, what he had heard had been true. When he found that it had, he told his family so – choosing to present the situation just as it had been presented to him. It was part, Henry said (alone, over his breakfast cereal, to practice the words before informing Owen and his father), of the greatest technological feat so far known to man. And marked (he added) an era of true progress, in which we (and now Henry looked up, at the table, still empty, nodding in the imagined directions of where his father and Owen would be) – evidently – have a part.

Owen and his grandfather were far less optimistic than Henry, and Henry, it turned out was less optimistic than he imagined himself to be. But, unlike his father, he was as resigned as he had been as a child, when it was his father who'd said *move*, and he'd picked up his pin and he'd moved.

¶People called the town "Casablanca" now. And while, like the rest of the residents, Henry packed silverware into boxes and watched angrily as the trees were cut down and the oldest houses burned (so that the field Henry's father had laboriously cleared could not in the end be differentiated from the rest of the landscape), Henry's father pursued a different course. At the beginning of July, in that last summer, Henry watched as his son followed his father back and forth from the gravel pits to haul buckets of coarse sand to the top of the yard where, when Jacqui had kept it, the garden had been.

There, his father marked the outline of his own dam, sticking in the uneven ground twelve mismatched spikes which would become (Henry's father assured Henry in the evenings), with the help of Owen's gravel and a system of loosely interlocked stones, a single, impenetrable wall.

The stones he rooted for himself from the new garden: a small plot at the front of the house, and also from the back, where a dilapidated stone fence snaked, half hidden in the grass.

Owen had been given the chore of hauling the gravel because it was a long walk to and from the pit, a mile each way. The days were hot and the wheelbarrow was so old that the wheel turned crookedly. On the return run the gravel tilted once in every rotation, nearly spilling each time, and clanging metal so sharply on metal that Owen's days – getting on now into the middle of July – were emblazoned long in his memory by the *click-clank*, *clickety-clank* of the wheelbarrow, which beat rhythmic as a drumbeat on the packed dirt road.

¶At first, Henry, observing the production from the kitchen window, had forbidden Owen to help.

"He's just gone a bit crazy, Owen, with the news," Henry told his son, while filling the feeders on the porch one day, and meeting Owen on the stair. "Don't you encourage him." Then, in sudden disgust at something he could not name, and perhaps at something of what he himself had said, he threw a handful of seeds violently into the yard.

The few birds, who had come shyly to watch, rose and scattered.

"Really," Henry said, composing himself again. "He should be used to it." He winked at Owen. "When I was a boy," he said, "we moved every week." But Owen didn't laugh as he might have at another time. And it occurred to Henry, for the first time, that he didn't know his son. Or have any idea what Owen could have been thinking then, or at all, during the many long hours of that summer that he had spent with the grandfather out in the yard.

Until then, Henry had only falsely assumed that the memories of his own childhood had been – imbued in the blood – passed on like a latent gene. But Owen of course, it occurred to Henry now, equally knew nothing of what his own life had been. Except, that is, for the map of the world.

"Now, just say flat-out no," Henry said, just to say something, though his conviction had wavered. "He'll forget about it soon enough, with any luck."

Then he turned his chair and wheeled it out along the porch to the second feeder, allowing Owen to pass. Chipping the hard bits of feed from the spout, where they'd jammed.

¶Still, Henry imagined that it might be easy again; that they might slide, get rid of the ghosts that they loved too well; move, maybe even farther afield. Settle in Toronto, maybe. Where Owen could go to the university, and they could live in a house with linoleum flooring, and no stairs (which in the old place his father was made to struggle with, up and down, each way, pausing for breath at each of the two narrow landings, his old black lungs startled by the thin air). There would be a backyard for himself and the birds. A small one, because he could not turn about in it, after all.

Owen could mow it himself, in a quarter of an hour.

¶Two weeks had gone by since Henry had first forbidden Owen to work on the dam, and Owen had only begun to work harder.

"He's crazy enough," Henry said one evening – trying again – as the two of them wrapped dishes together in the kitchen. "Now this is too much. If they can sink a town, they can certainly sink a half-built fence. It wouldn't even keep a goat out."

Owen, who had been standing on a high stool, reaching into the far recesses of the old cabinets, nodded, passing Henry a gravy tureen.

After a while, Henry didn't mention it anymore.

2 That night after the meal, Henry pushed from the table. "Save your fork," he said, "there may be pie," then he let his own knife and fork rain down on his plate, making a loud clattering noise. My father repeated those last words, "May be pie, yep," as Henry wheeled himself into the other room, as if agreeing with something. But it didn't ever mean anything when Henry said that. It was just an old expression of his or a joke whose origin everyone had forgotten by then. We hardly heard him when he

said it, and there rarely was, if ever, pie to eat in that house after any meal. Sometimes Susan, the nurse, would bring some dessert down, or once in a while my father would pick up a flat store-bought pie that no one was ever thrilled about. It's the dimensions of a pie, after all, that can be, when they are, so satisfying. Those flat pies would just sit on the counter for a while uneaten, until, that summer, I threw them out.

I wondered what they'd done when I wasn't around to throw out all the food that spoiled.

¶By that time Henry was settled, with his notebook, in the other room. We could hear the click of the television and then the low roar of the game on. My father and I remained, without speaking, working on our own puzzle: the still as-yet-unsolved crossword of the day before.

It wasn't until the game was over, and Henry had wheeled himself from the TV to his adjacent bedroom, and we heard the final grunt of his last push-up against the ledge of the bed – seven of which he orchestrated nightly with the diligence and raptness of prayer – that my father, with his good hand in the air, his finger raised and pointed to the ceiling as if he too had stumbled upon a moment of divine inspiration, announced that the puzzle was complete.

¶The next morning, when the telephone rang, my father lunged for it, thinking it was Helen, but it was the hospital instead. As we drove across the border that afternoon, my father stared out the window in the same relative silence, unusual to him, as he had coming back that way the week before.

This time, though, when he caught me looking as I drove, he would lean over to pat my knee, smiling wanly, saying something like, "Watcha thinking, Honey," without expecting a reply. I believe he felt sorry for me.

The x-ray, which had been taken of my father's shoulder the week before, had illuminated a large mass in his right lung, and though he was sent from test to test all afternoon, as I waited, reading magazines in the empty hospital hall, each test (due, they said, to a general deterioration of the lung) came back "inconclusive." And so, although it was assumed that my father had, by that particular day in June, progressed into the late stages of an aggressive lung cancer, we were sent away, in the end, without a diagnosis.

¶That night my father drank his first beer since Fargo. It had been thirteen years. Then he drank twelve more. "Let's not be so fucking morose around here," is what he said, when he opened up the third can.

I left the house and walked down to the dock. I didn't want to be outside, but I didn't want to be inside either. I stood for as long as I could down there, concentrating on a small point of light on the opposite shore. Then, because I could think of nothing else, I turned and followed the familiar beam of Henry's own porch light back up to the government house.

The possibilities of a life, it seemed, were small.

At first, as I made my way from the dock, Henry's light too appeared like a distant star – one that was perhaps already dead – but then, as I moved closer, up the hill and away from the water, it became a large animal eye, and then, bigger than that, a star again. Only this time very vibrant, certainly living. And then it was just what it was: a lamp, glowing on the outside rail.

My father was on his fifth beer when I returned. Henry saw me first and gave me a look, and his look said, *What can I do.* So I looked back. Nothing.

I sat down at the table across from Henry and picked up the day's crossword, but it was already complete.

Henry was, for once, not watching the game, but he had his notebook out still, and once or twice he glanced at it, but he did not seem to be working on anything. After a while, my father, who really was in a jovial mood – certainly not morose – and who would continue to be until his thirteenth beer felled him, said, "Well, Henry, what d'ye got?"

Henry shrugged. "Nothing yet."

My father moved to the fridge where he opened a sixth can.

"Did I ever tell you, Honey, how it was that Paul Erdos here," and he leaned around to slap Henry on the shoulder, "saved my life?"

"Who?" I said.

"Erdos!" My father shouted, and sat down at the table. "You haven't saved the world yet," he said to Henry, who smiled, and to hide the smile bent again as though to work in earnest at a problem that did not seem to be actually written on the page. "You got to start somewhere, though," my father said, "don't you? You got to start someplace."

"Who's Erdos?" I asked.

My father coughed out a laugh and pointed with his good arm at Henry again. "You're looking at him!" he said. "Okay," I said. And picked up the paper again, though there was still nothing to read.

My father did not give up so easily, though, and so he told me this story, just as he had been intending to do all along.

¶"I was God knows where," he said. "Some awful town halfway between the coast and Fargo. Sick. Sick, drunk, and doing this puzzle at a crummy hotel. And I'm almost done. There's just this one clue left, this one goddamn clue, I'll never forget. 'The man who loved numbers' it was, and I'm thinking, dammit, I *know that guy*, that's Henry."

"He tried plugging that in there," Henry said. "Right amount. Wrong letters."

"I just had this five-letter word," my father continued, "with an 'e' and a 'd' and an 'o' at random, and that didn't mean shit to me! I was so close, almost done the damn thing, and there was just that one little word, just two letters really, in the whole damn thing that I was missing, so I stumbled down to the front desk and I said, *Excuse me, but — would you — mind — looking something up?*"

Henry laughed a little at this, in an under-his-breath kind of way. It was encouragement enough for my father to roar out his own laugh, which was checked by a cough. "It was damn funny," he agreed, "drunk as a skunk and this nice girl saying, *Certainly, sir, what can I do for you?* and so then I told her and she said, *I'm sorry —*" my father changed his voice in mockery of her high-pitched tone. "I'm *sorry, sir, but I don't think I have that cape — a — bility.*"

"Yes, you do," my father said, and leaned over the counter to look at her computer. "You've got the Internet there, don't you –"

"Well yes, sir, but it's only for searching out hotels and business-related sites," she said in her clipped, official way.

"Well, they make you swear on a bible before they give you this lousy job, or what?"

"You're drunk, sir," she said. "I'm going to have to ask you to return to your room, or else I'll need to call the manager."

My father collected himself. "Look," he said, "I'm sorry. I just really need this information. You'd be doing me a *huge*, just a huge favour. If you could just search for this piece of information. It really won't take a minute."

The girl looked around a moment and fidgeted in her chair. "Okay," she said. "What is it?"

"Oh, good," my father said. "Okay, this is good. Just could you type 'the man who loves numbers' right in the box? See if it works."

The girl clicked that into her computer. Her mouth a tight line, pinched in at the corners.

"Okay, we've got like a zillion sites here," she said. "Well, what for?"

"We got, 'the man who loves only numbers is easy to love ...'"

"Keep going ..."

"Despite his strangeness ... Paul Erdos, 19 –"

"Wait, go back, how do you spell that name – what you just said."

"Paul Erdos," she said. "E–r–d–o–s."

My father was counting the letters out on his hand, very deliberately, like a child.

"That's it!" he said. "Erdos. Thank you."

¶Later, my father went to the library and looked Erdos up. "He *was* strange," he said. "Completely dysfunctional. Couldn't ever keep an apartment. He was always crashing at this or that place, friends of his, friends of friends. But the thing was, no one cared about it. Everyone just loved to have the guy around because he was such a genius. Really, the guy was brilliant. All he cared about was math. He would sit around for hours, just like our resident genius here, and come up with problems, and then solve them, and that was all there was to life for him. That was the one thing he thought was worth a damn."

"So, wait," I said. "How did he save your life?"
"Oh, well," my father said, and I realized that claiming that at the beginning had only been a narrative device, a hook to pull me into his story about this Erdos, who was so funny to him, but about whom otherwise I would have cared only marginally.

"Well," Henry put in to help him out, where my father had hesitated, "he calls me on the phone one day, just right out of the blue, and starts going off, telling me, like he told you, about this Erdos fella, and how we were, Erdos and I, I mean, just alike. And he talks so long to me on the phone, and I haven't seen him, or heard from him in so many years as you know, so finally the only thing I can think to do t'get him off the phone, stop talking my ear off, you know, was say, Now why the hell don't you just come on back now?"

"And so I started driving back that night," my father said. "Didn't know why it'd taken me so long. Kept thinking I'd clean myself up but then it didn't matter. All the sudden I just wanted more than anything else to be at the lake, and with you kids, and Henry, like it was when —"

My father paused and Henry rolled his chair back from the table and then forward again. It was a nervous sort of motion, and served to distract everyone, as it was meant to, from the sudden thickness in my father's voice.

"But when was that?" I asked, "That wasn't that one summer was it? Your first summer back?"

As far as I knew the first time that my father returned to the lake after his disappearance he had been sober for some months.

"No," my father said, his melancholy suddenly abandoned. "Cops picked me up that night coming into Fargo, and I got another DUI which landed me in rehab, and then in the hospital because that didn't work. Nearly busted my gut for good in an effort of retaliation. Then rehab again, and that time it stuck. It was the following summer that I finally made it back out here."

"So Paul Erdos really didn't have anything to do with it at all," I said. "In fact, he could have killed you, not saved your life. If the cops hadn't picked you up just then, I mean."

"I can't owe my life to a couple of West Fargo cops!" my father roared. "Innit better I owe it to our Henry here?"

"Not me," Henry said. "My name didn't fit, remember?"

"Paul Er—dos," my father said, relishing each syllable, "to whom I owe the rest of my days —"

"A good man, a maths man," Henry agreed.

"And the best part, the best part," my father said, "the wisest words any a man spoke."

"Oh, gawd," said Henry, who had evidently heard all this before.

"First," my father said, adopting a theatrical pose, and deepening his voice so that it rang out in the little kitchen, making the room seem suddenly quite barren and small, "First you forget to zip up, and then you forget to zip down. That's poetry," he said.

"That's depressing," I said.

"You're depressed," Henry said. "This man saved his life for it."

"First you forget to zip up ..." my father said, "and then ..."

"Put a lid on it," Henry said. "We heard you the first time." And then, to change the subject, he continued with his own story.

3 As soon as the ground thawed in the spring, Owen and his grandfather continued their work on the backyard dam. It was necessary to reconstruct the scaffolding in the places where, over the winter, it had crumbled. This time, they were able to use the sticks and brush from the trees the power company had felled in the previous fall, eliminating the landscape.

Gradually it began to dawn on Henry that his father had, quite simply, gone mad.

It was not only the grandfather who had refused to go, but it was the grandfather who stayed longest – who, even after Henry and Owen had relocated to the newly built government house off the lake road, continued, without Owen's help now, to work on the backyard dam. So that every day, for four weeks, until they were no longer permitted to do so, Henry and Owen drove the six miles back to the house, in order to ask the grandfather to return with them to town.

"It won't work, Granddad. I seen the dam," said Owen.

Each time, equally, they were refused.

When the water began to rise, and still Henry's father and two other residents remained, the police intervened: they came around in a borrowed boat and picked everyone up like it was a carpool. Owen went along. He sat beside Henry and two of the officers in the bow, and so was the first to notice his grandfather from some distance away. How he was standing, his hands by his sides, on the porch, where the water had now reached the uppermost step, wetting his shoes. One of the officers leaned forward, causing the boat to lilt heavily to one side. He winked at Owen, and handed him the megaphone, which turned out to be surprisingly heavy in his hand. Then, though he hardly knew that he had spoken, Owen heard his own voice, scattered and exaggerated in the air.

When finally the grandfather stepped from the porch over the boat's rail, he held Owen's shoulder in order to steady himself, and then – as though it was an umbrella in heavy wind, and unaware that he did so – he continued to hold it, long after he had settled next to Henry and Owen on a low bench in the bow.

4 While my father drank and did crosswords and watched rented DVDs up at the house, I began to spend more and more time down at the water, with Henry. We'd take the boat out and, as in my childhood, spend the days putting in and around the coves, or on still days, just sit for hours out in the middle of the lake with Henry's fishing line dropped straight down, though he never seemed to catch anything that way.

When I was younger, and we had come to Henry's house alone in those solitary summers of my father's disappearance, I had imagined that the past really existed, semi-submerged, in Henry's backyard. Wouldn't that be enough for anyone? I'd thought. To explain that certain sadness, which I identified sometimes in him. A sadness that would make you, when you saw it, want to pull the edges of your own life up around you, and stay there, carefully, inside.

Now, though, I find it difficult to believe that anything is ever buried in the way that I had once supposed. I believe instead that everything remains. At the very limit; the exact surface of things. So that in the end it is not so much what has been subtracted from a life that really matters, but the distances, instead, between the things which remain.

¶It was always a bit of a thing getting Henry into the boat from his chair, but then he was so happy there, and seemed more comfortable, his thin legs folded beneath him, where he did not need them. Occasionally, he would reach out an arm and bark out for me to stop if I was the one driving, and then we would just float a bit on the water and look around and we would stay very quiet together for a while, like that. We didn't talk about my father, or the fact that he was dying. Or about Helen, and how angry she had been that he was drinking again. How she had spat fiercely at me over the phone, *Why don't you do something?*

Or about my own life, and the things that I had and had not left behind, and whether or not I would find some other sort of life now, and what sort of life that would be.

I didn't ask Henry any questions on our trips, as I did sometimes in the evenings when he told me stories, and he didn't ask me any either.

There were questions I would have liked to ask, though, and sometimes I'd wondered them aloud to my father or to Helen. Why Henry had never married again, for example. And, of course, about Owen.

Once my father said, women think that they can make sad things go away by knowing the reason that they happened. This was in dismissal of a question that I asked him once about his experiences in the war. He told me that in my curiosity I was just like my mother, and in the tone that he said it I knew that at that moment it was the worst thing of all.

So I never mentioned the war to him again, until those many years later, when he told me himself.

I did believe that, I guess. That I could *make sad things go away.* Believed that if I knew what had happened to Henry (he had never spoken until that summer of his accident) that I could prevent an accident like that ever happening to myself, or to any of the people I loved.

Believed, I suppose, that if there was a precise reason

that I could get hold of to explain why Henry, and both of my parents ended up so very much alone, that I could prevent, for myself, an equivalent loneliness.

For the most part, though, I was more or less content in those days: sitting out with Henry on the lake. Cutting the motor when he asked me to, and drifting in silence with him. Hauling up the outboard when we passed over the old foundations, and dropping long lines into the water with heavy sinkers to catch nothing, even in a long afternoon.

My own sadness seemed, at those times, to draw itself in – a complete and separate object – so that it seemed to have nothing to do with me anymore. Just as Henry's sadness seemed, on those afternoons, to have very little to do with him, and the things I had always supposed to be its source. We floated over the old town with such ease, after all, and I sensed not even the smallest regret in Henry then. No, it was not the lost town, or even, it seemed, the details of his life since – even the horribly sad things – that his sadness had to do with. All of it had happened so long ago, and it's true that people, as Henry said himself, *get on with things*. With greater or lesser degrees of success, but anyway, get on with things, after long periods of time like that.

No, it had to do, instead, I think – that sadness – with those certain smells or shapes or colours that call up a moment, or a feeling, just a whiff of one, that you can't quite place. Just something that fills you with a weird longing, all of a sudden. Like you're homesick. Only not for any place that you've been to. And the smell, it doesn't

83

remind you of anything that you've ever smelled before. And the colour or the shape is not one you can connect to a recallable landscape.

5 Then, in the middle of July, I woke once more to the sounds of my father's primeval shouts. They travelled up the two flights of stairs to Owen's third-floor room as before, but this time there was a different sort of urgency that I heard in my father's voice. An echo of something, almost forgotten. As though whatever it was had reverberated there in his lungs for many years, only now to reach me.

When, some time later, I joined Henry and my father in the kitchen, I saw that there was a book out on the table in the place where a crossword would otherwise have been. When he saw me, my father gave another quick whoop and a shout and opened the book to the page that he had marked with his thumb – an illustration of *The Petrel* – and I knew then that it was the boat that had remained, echoing in my father all those years, and which he once again wanted to begin.

¶The boat had continued to live – ever since the day my mother had removed it from Roddy Stewart's shed in Mexico, paid him the fifty dollars in cash that he figured he was owed, and driven it to Orono, an hour and a half away – at my grandmother's house. So that for the intervening eighteen years, until my father pointed to it as though at random in the open pages of a book, the boat had sat in my grandmother's barn at the end of the dirt track of the drive, just the way that it had sat before, in Roddy Stewart's shed. Only there, it was shat upon by so many generations of pigeons that it appeared as though it had indeed been a seagoing vessel, covered in tough barnacles from head to toe. Because nothing at my grandmother's house had ever finally, or irreversibly, been thrown out, the barn served as the last resting place for many items of little, or suspended, meaning, and the boat became for me, like the other objects (the several generations' worth of discarded bicycles, unusable furniture and ruined lumber), a rare artifact; as though it existed, disembodied from human origin, in a separate, more probable world of its own.

I think that I forgot, in fact, the way that boat was connected to my family at all. The way it had seemed at one time to tear my mother in two, and received from her both the fierce anger and pride which she also bestowed upon Helen and me. Because no one but myself ever went up to the barn, except to deposit more objects into the growing collection, I was able to establish the boat in my own, more private and less complicated system; I don't think I even realized that it was unfinished. To me, it was enough that the boat existed there, unused, in our barn. That it was shat upon by generations of pigeons. That it sailed only in my imagination.

I would be surprised, for example, to hear my mother speak offhandedly one day of the boat's eventual completion.

"Why else do you think," she said, "that we kept it all these years!" Not realizing that I had long given up, if it had ever existed in me, the sense that grown-up people did or did not do things for particular reasons.

I was not a child anymore at the time that my mother spoke of finishing the boat. My father had resurfaced; I believe I was nearly twenty. And though I did not ask my mother about the other articles that had been left in the barn, in a flash I imagined the whole collection of defunct lawn furniture, sofa beds and unserviceable engine parts, after years of idleness and dehabilitation, springing suddenly to life.

"Your grandmother always wished that I would just throw it out," my mother said to me once, incredulously. And there appeared again that same look that often had appeared in her eye when speaking to Helen or me. In which, even in the semi-moment of its inception, we felt ourselves to be so extraordinarily loved that it took the breath out of us all at once, in a rush. Shot through with an affection so fierce that it mingled in us with an equivalent sense of terror: at the amount that we had already taken from her, and also from the world, which we feared we would never quite be able, or even willing, to return.

I hope that now, when I go on to say that my father – having leaned from the book and removed his finger from the page that I now held open, having given a loud guffaw, followed by a low cough – then rose from the table in order to telephone my mother, it will be in some way understood, the vast and irremediable wound that we inflicted on her in that summer, my father's last, when we extracted the boat from my grandmother's barn and drove it north to Casablanca.

It had been a surprise to learn that the boat had also remained, for my father, linked to the initial promise with which it had been born. He had never spoken to us of the

boat, except in passing, and because of this I had, I suppose, always assumed that for him, as for me, any tangible
notion of the boat's completion had been relegated to the
distant and unrecoverable past.

My mother's protestations went unheeded. I – and even
Helen, though she was still hardly speaking to him – took
my father's side. I think now that we even hoped with the
boat, even in the idea of it, to replace my father's Fargo
palace, for which we felt accountable somehow.

It's funny, isn't it? The way that we always position
ourselves at the centre of our own stories, and that even
from some distance – even relegated to the third person,
and, from the present tense at least two times removed –
we continue to imagine ourselves in that way. It shouldn't,
for example, have taken me so many years to realize that
what I had for so long referred to as my father's boat was
indeed my father's boat; far more so anyway than it ever
had been – or would be – mine.

Or taken still more years to realize that it was far less
his than it was my mother's; built as it had been out of an
extraordinary love for her, which had continued, throughout everything, and was why, after all those years, he had
thought of the boat at all.

Or, similarly, that the story that I was telling was not my
own. That I would never be able to understand it – not my
own life, and certainly not the lives of others – because
even the simplest things appeared to me to be the most
complicated puzzles, for which I had only the most inad-
equate of clues. And that, by reading backwards along the
lives of objects, and the things that I had learned piecemeal
from my parents, and from the rest of the world, I was

only being thrown farther and farther off course, and was by now very far from the straight and deep waters for which I had always felt I was somehow bound. And that, each time I'd thought I was coming closer to that unknown region I desired, I was actually following an altogether different route; a small estuary quite sideways to that true course of things, ending up in distant and uncomfortable regions I had never dreamed of visiting before.

Is it only now, through aggravation at the continued frustration of my attempts, or is it an accidental wisdom that somehow I've acquired? Which leads me finally to believe that the small estuaries to which I have been blown are just as true as the rest, and that the deep and open and still untried waters have been left uncharted because they do not in fact exist at all; except, that is, in the magic lantern pictures of my mind where they are just a simple shadow-play of death, which someday, and far too soon, will have us all freely sailing there.

6 On the day the boat was taken from the barn, Helen and I climbed into the upper loft where, years before, it had been relegated in order to afford room below for the increasing number of objects which collected there. With the help of two neighbours, along with my father, who wheezed in the wings and shouted directions to us through the barn's wide doors, we lowered the boat very slowly to the ground. From there we were able to move it easily onto Henry's old boat trailer, which we had borrowed for the occasion, and there it roosted, after having made the effort on untried wings and after many years:

outdoors. As though it had never doubted itself at all. As though it had, in fact, very little to do with my father, or even with my mother, who sat fuming in the kitchen, in order that she would not cry. As though it had nothing to do with human beings at all. With keeping things, or not keeping things. With patterns, or with the systems of memory that we construct: the arrangement of object to object, one against the other, in our lives.

My father, as he leaned against the boat, catching his breath for the thousandth time, looked as though he were a hundred years old. So small, suddenly, beside the boat that everything seemed reversed somehow. As if it was the boat that had been waiting for him, and not he for it. And it was only at that moment that I realized. That I felt it, in the pit of my belly, as if it were my own: the great wound that was opening in my mother's heart, as my father caught his breath and leaned against the boat's side, and my sister Helen tied the straps to the boat with panache, and Henry, looming from his chair by the car door, surveyed everything with unquiet eyes, as though sensing something in the wind.

¶Helen, with her practical sense of things, had, throughout the weeks of a lingering feud, said only, "This is driving me crazy. It's a fucking boat." Not realizing, or choosing to overlook, that the heart of the matter lay in that very thing: that it was not the significance, but rather that the boat failed to signify anything at all that really mattered. That it had come, that is, for my mother, to represent through its very blankness that secret, unknown quantity with which she had one day hoped to solve the problem of our lives.

But there was no formula that day, and even my sadness I kept to myself and did not allow to blend or to combine in any way: with the sadnesses of my mother, for example – also isolate – as she came out bravely from the house and walked to the end of the drive, to stand beside the window and to kiss my father on the lips, with tears standing in her eyes, though she did not acknowledge them; that by not brushing them away she perhaps intended were not there.

Thinking all that time, not now of the boat, which had perhaps in this moment realized most completely what my sister and I had hoped for it – its object-ness – but of my father, who was suddenly, unbearably, old. And that, in all probability, it had come only to this, that this was the ultimate reach of the story which they had made of their lives. That no matter how variously they had dreamt the end, it had arrived, and there was nothing to be undone, and nothing to be retained.

Or of the sadnesses of my father. Who, though he was in a jovial mood (slapping Henry on the back, and opening his third can of beer that morning, after my mother had stepped back from the car), must have contained it as well.

No, it was only a small and a personal sadness which I harboured in me then, I could do no better. A sadness which could at that time have no outlet, because of the position that we had taken, Helen and I: that it would be possible for the boat to be reduced in such a way, to its object form, alleviated of twenty-five years and all they had contained. Of the great and always ill-fitting imposition of meaning on form. That it could be set free, as we ourselves on that afternoon believed that we might be. As

Helen snapped pictures of the boat disappearing from the dirt track of my grandmother's road, and Henry and my father and I began our drive away – from the safety of my mother's keeping – all the way to Ontario, and the boat's bow puffed like the throat of a bird who, in lifting itself from the ground, had already forgotten that it had ever been held there, and had cut all ties.

¶We arrived back at the government house on a Tuesday, but it wasn't until Friday afternoon that we managed finally to transfer the boat from the trailer into Henry's garage. Following my father's instructions, we constructed two blocks on which the boat could rest, and from which position it would be possible to properly begin.

It took us those three whole days just to get the boat off the ground, and when we did my father celebrated by drinking eight beers in a row, and falling into a semi-coma, slumped over at the kitchen table.

On the fourth day, he did not get out of bed at all, and later in the afternoon telephoned Gerry in Fargo.

"Well, it's time, old man," I heard him say.

Gerry, as well as being my father's sponsor and long-time friend, had also been a carpenter and had worked with my father over many years, and in that time they had often spoken together of completing the boat one day. But I knew nothing of this at the time and heard only my father's lingering pause as the unprecedented Gerry – in an unintelligible tongue (which sounded, through the telephone line, like a low electric hum) – mysteriously entered the story. Heard my father, the interpreter of mysteries, decipherer of unfamiliar tongues, say, "No look, it's just going to sit around here, really. If you can make it out, it's yours."

And just like that, my father took the boat away from us, just as my mother had said that he would.

¶In truth, there was a part of me that was relieved. The boat had been, in this way, given up before I myself might be required to do so. But still, there was another part of me which felt a bit like how, I might imagine now, my mother felt on the day the boat was uprooted from the barn. Or like Owen had, when one day he'd told his grandfather that he'd given up the dam, as though it was he himself, in his complicity, who had let the water in.

Neither my father nor my mother had any idea where the original blueprints for The Petrel, which I had thought to be so extraordinary in my childhood, had disappeared to – but without too much trouble my father managed to locate the same plans on the Internet and printed them off. For weeks, even before the boat itself arrived, and until the project was halted with my father's telephone call, we had gazed on them. To me, their intricate delineations seemed to express a form more exquisite, and consisting of many more dimensions, than the simple diagram of the completed Petrel, which had been drawn into my father's book. Or than would later be indicated to me as a possibility by the hull that sat, untouched, on its wooden blocks where Henry and I had lifted it – waiting all through the rest of that final summer for a fourth, and peripheral, character, to take it away.

But even then my father, always a house carpenter, did not admit defeat.

"Gerry'll fix it up in no time," he said. "You bet. Then we'll all go out together. Sail it out on Grass Lake. Take your mother along."

7 After the boat was abandoned, my father got out of bed later and later each day. Sometimes he would not get up at all, but would stay in bed, not eating, listening to the radio and cursing the news reports; the curtains closed.

At three o'clock in the afternoon, on a day like that in mid-August, Henry wheeled himself into the closed bedroom and flicked on the overhead light.

"What the hell's the matter with you?" Henry said.

"It's the damn morphine," Henry complained when he'd returned to the kitchen. "He shouldn't take so much of it. Not with all that bloody alcohol."

¶My father's energy would return briefly, however, even in those days, by late afternoon, and then he would argue politics with Henry more fervently than he had in the past – his head full of radio reports. So that even when Henry tried to cut him short ("I don't like disturbances in my place," he'd growl), my father would argue on, right past the Bogart line, until Henry said, "If it was up to you we'd all be frickin' communists," which was an improvisation of his own, and set my father really going.

I didn't mind the debates. They reminded me, as they seemed to remind my father, that he was still alive, and, because they gave a direction to an anger that seemed to rise so readily in him in those days, and which otherwise did not seem to be directed at anything at all, they were something of a relief.

My father might yell, for example, "Godammit!" in the middle of a meal, and it would turn out to be the simplest thing that was the matter. His salad, which had fallen from his fork, say; as simple as that.

At those times, I would say to my father, "*What's wrong?*" with such concern, that he would have no choice but to apologize.

"Oh nothing, it's just this salad," he'd say. "It won't stay on the goddamn fork."

"Eat with yer hands," Henry would say. "That's what the communists do."

¶I would take Henry's car out sometimes and drive into town, just because I had nothing else to do. Then I'd stop at the grocery store, even though we never seemed to need anything. I liked the way that everything was so clean in there, and lit up as if from the inside, so that, though of course cluttered with many bright objects, it always appeared quite bare. Also, I liked the way that you could drift around in there with the other shoppers, in slow patterns, like birds, listening together to the constant hum of the music on the radio, which we hardly heard. Until, that is, a voice, in an authoritative burst, would interrupt to inspire within us a shared desire, which otherwise we could not have identified as our own.

I never came home empty-handed.

"Oh, good," my father said, one time when I chose mustard, and placed it on the kitchen table like I'd brought flowers. "Good thinking." He was a fan of Dijon mustard because it was something he could taste.

I would make him sandwiches which he barely touched, and when I complained, or worse, sat glumly at the end of his bed, unspeaking, my father would rouse himself to say, "Don't you worry, my sweetheart."

"After all," he said once, in his best Bogart voice, leaning forward to give my shoulder a second-rate squeeze, "I came to Casablanca for my health."

I did not feel up to it then, but it was clear that my father had felt even less up to it than I. So I said: "I often speculated on why you didn't return to America."

It was, on my part, a very weak Renault, but my father did not complain, and continued to look at me expectantly, waiting for the line to follow.

"Did you abscond with the church funds?" I added, and this time I managed a deep voice, clipped and official, which made my father laugh.

He repeated his original line, and then continued. "I came to Casablanca for the waters."

"What waters?" I said. "We're in the desert."

His Bogart face was set, solemn and impassive: "I was misinformed."

8 One afternoon, I took the boat out on my own, to the far end of the disappearing road, where Henry's old place would have been. I stopped there, letting the boat drift slightly. Then I lay back on a pile of life jackets so that my head rested on the deck of the bow. I imagined

the house, below me, still standing, like the old dock of the film. And the dam, too, that the grandfather built: still holding some things in and some things out.

It's funny to think about. The way the whole world is disappearing like that. That every moment we get closer, until – and inevitably – there comes that one instant, that impetus, whatever it will be, by which we are one day blown, finally, from our own furthest extremity. Like leaves from a thin branch at the end of a tree.

Inevitably: that much I was able to know. And so I said that word to myself, exactly, out loud. But I was, in saying it, acting against myself. I wanted instead to cover my ears, or whatever it was that listened to me when I spoke inside my head. And also my heart. Cover that. If that's, after all, what the feeling part of me was.

But, as I floated over Henry's old house, and did not listen to myself, it occurred to me that the reverse of the thing was also as true. That instead of disappearing – or equally, as we disappeared – we also existed more heavily, in layers. And that by remaining, as in floodwater, always at the surface of everything, though our points of reference begin to slowly change, it is always so slight a transition, moment to moment, that it is almost always imperceptible.

So that, in coming to live as we do at such a far remove from ourselves, it becomes possible – no, unavoidable at times – to float over certain essential objects without noticing them at all. As just in that moment, for example, I in Henry's boat bobbed above Henry's old house – from which vantage point I might have seen, if unobstructed, all the way down to the ruins of the grandfather's dam below.

Time, it seemed – at once material, at once not – existed there, in that in-between: in the way that I might have, but could not, see down. In the way that I continued only to be suspended, at some distance, by that most curious of elements: an ultra-density of air. Removed always by a thickness to things.

Everything exists like that. Doesn't it. Always in further combination, like the objects of my grandmother's barn. Or like my father's boat, which likewise, with time, did not diminish or disappear, but only lengthened and lengthened, until it had stretched itself into an irreducible oblivion, doggedly pursuing itself along an always advancing and invisible line.

¶I had by that time drifted so near shore that the boat snagged on a rock and jarred heavily so that waves began to knock it repeatedly, sometimes splashing over the side. I got out to push myself off, getting wet to the knee. Then I started back to the government house.

Twice I glanced behind me as I went, but each time when I looked back I realized that I could do no more than I had already done. No more commit that place to memory, or understand. And so, finally, I gave it up. Having realized nothing, and felt very little, I had only to turn the boat around, resolutely, in the way that I had come.

¶Later that evening, as we sat together in my father's bedroom, a DVD playing on the TV that had been moved in there, but the sound turned off, I asked: "Why did Owen go to the war when he didn't have to?"

My father looked at me, as though he had only just then realized I was in the room. "Hello, my sweetheart," he said.

It was late, and my father's speech was slurred by morphine and beer. On the TV screen the light flickered through an unknown city, and a man, chased by another man, ran endlessly, and at odd angles, through the shifting streets.

I thought that he hadn't heard the question, but I didn't repeat it. I sat down next to him on the bed, and squeezed his hand, which was smaller than I had remembered, and even more exactly like Helen's. Already, it seemed to be losing the rough edges of itself, which had made it his own, its evidence of contact with the world.

We watched the screen a while longer. The city – soundless – continued to enter the room in flashes, the light cut by the sharp angles of the tall glass buildings, all eyes.

"Nobody," my father said, "has to do anything that they don't want to do. You should know that." His voice wavered, an underwater sound.

"But, I mean," I said, quickly. "It was different with you. With the draft –" I let my voice break off.

My father looked at me. As though it was me, suspended at a just imaginable distance to himself, who was going to tell him something then. But finally, very simply, as though he had not doubted it, he said: "I joined up too." Then blew his nose furiously, and asked me to open up another can of beer from the fridge.

I went out into the cool kitchen, and returned, handing him a beer.

"You did?" I asked.

But again it appeared that my father had not heard.

¶Some time later, however, as I was clearing the dishes – which always lingered long after any meal – my father, speaking loudly from his bedroom, where he had lately retired, said: "You know, if you want to know something about the war, I should tell you about my brother, Clark."

¶It is strange to stumble upon something which you have believed for so long to have been lost that you don't even find it missing anymore. As though, having repeatedly tripped in the darkness against a final imaginary stair, one day you find it underfoot again as if it had been there all along.

At first, though, my father told me very little about the war, and I am still unsure of why, when he first spoke of it, he spoke of his brother Clark, with whom he had never been close, and whose "tragedy" – as my father described it – seemed to have very little to do with the war, or with my father. I guess it was only that I hadn't expected that the great and undiscoverable quantity, which we had for so long assumed to exist at the root, would have anything to do with my Uncle Clark, who lived somewhere in Minnesota, worked in a sporting-goods store, and had got my father into Internet trading. Who, every year, sent a Christmas card with a picture of himself and his dog inside, on the back of which was always scribbled, "With love from two Minnesota Mutts."

But of course it did. And still, my father's sadness when he spoke of his brother's life was far more evident than, when pressed, he talked of his own, and I think now that perhaps it is always easier that way. To understand the grief of another, instead of our own. Because of the way that we are able, then, to hold it at some distance from ourselves and have it return to us – in its thousand reflective eyes – not only our own otherwise unperceivable image, but also our manner of looking at the world; splitting it into a thousand directions.

Vietnam

1967

With Olaf it is different. He must give up not merely his life but also the good name that valiance customarily wins, the hero's renown and reputation ... He can do so lightly, however, defying both the military force of his nation and its massively conformed opinions, because he answers to an individual rather than a collective truth.

GARY LANE

1 The quarter of a joint that he smokes in late morning helps, so that, with the heat, he is again a small child. Sick in bed, with a fever; his mother, even now. If he listens he can hear it. Padding, padding down the corridor, her sock-feet on the floor.

That's what it feels like, anyway.

If the door opens, it is his forehead, also opening.

"Napoleon?" his mother asks.

¶They are all very serious about it, and Owen always rolls. The other three gather to watch. They want to make sure that he rolls it out even. That the tobacco doesn't gravitate to the rear of the joint, and that it doesn't narrow at the end. Teddy always smokes first, and all eyes are on him as he begins. His tongue on the paper, in and out, then in and out again. He looks, in between the dartings of his tongue, up, at each one of them in turn. Then he holds the match out away from the joint and brings it down, between his teeth, slowly to the flame. He is careful so that it doesn't burn too fast.

In Danang they can smoke the shit out of this stuff. There, they often found themselves staring into their own laps in a stubborn disbelief, confused to find themselves still attached to their own bodies, and in that way to the ground. Sometimes they'd collapse, and pound on the ground, and laugh, and say, "That's so *fucked*, that's so fucked," because they were exactly where they were and nowhere else. And just by saying it – "That's so fucked, isn't it fucked?" – they knew or thought they knew that they were talking about the same thing, which, at that time or perhaps at any other, they could not have begun to explain.

Now it has to be just this taste, these five drags each, and in the late morning they gather. Teddy loves lighting the joint because of the attention he gets. He works on perfecting the particular tilt of his head when he first really hauls on the thing. On the way he half closes his eyes.

Napoleon comes after Teddy. If he forgets himself and takes too much he will feel his throat catch on the smoke and wind up spitting most of it out, spluttering it through his mouth and his nose. Plus, it isn't fair to do that. They watch every haul, and get five pretty long ones each – which is twenty in total – maybe twenty-one if Owen, who finishes it off, can stand it, and goes in, burning his lips and fingers on the end, after a final draw. They watch partially to make sure that no one takes more than their fair share but partially for the sheer pleasure of it; liking especially the moments in which each man's breath is held.

After a while the eyes start to bulge, and there's a small gurgle at the back of the throat. The rest of them hold their breaths, too, but they don't even notice that they do this. They hardly pay attention to themselves at all and so it is only the man with the smoke in his lung's heart that is heard for the entire duration of the held-in breath.

Hill, surprisingly, because he's the runt of the group, can hold his breath longest.

The heat stretches it out so that Napoleon can feel the effects almost all afternoon. He is in this way a sick boy in

bed, waiting for his mother to pad down the hall, for most
of his first assignment.

¶Lieutenant Bean is a clean-cut, upbeat man from Indiana,
and although he keeps himself aloof and is not gentle with
them, he sometimes relaxes into moments of near friend-
ship. Like when they smoke their cigarettes together after
a meal, and he says "This isn't Virginia or wherever you
little fucks did your training, ye may have figgered that out
by now." And laughs good-naturedly, leaning back on his
pack. Sweeping his arm around him in a ring.

One time he tells them about his own first tour. "It was
fuckin' scary, I can tell you that," he says. "If only so's you
know how lucky you are now. A few weeks of pure fuckin'
hell," he says. "Officers just little dipshits like yourselves,
fresh from California. Didn't know the first thing about
combat. Didn't know that –"

But Teddy interrupts him, grinning. "This isn't fucking
California," he says. Happily, Bean is not angry, but laughs.

"That's right," he says, slapping Teddy on the back.
"But I'm serious," he tells them. "You boys haven't seen
anything like it, and you won't. You can count your pretty
fuckin' stars too. All the time, *boom bam*, mines everywhere.
We were scared like rabbits. Nobody knew where to shoot
– the F.O. was fucked, our coordinates were off half the
time – and the gooks would be everywhere, so we didn't
know. Were we hitting them, or were we blowing up our
own guys?"

He shifts his neck on his pack and clears his throat again,
and no one says anything. "But that's all different now,
thank Christ," Bean tells them. "You guys are lucky in a way,

bouncing in here at the end of the war. It's gonna be cake for you – just these last assignments, just this cleaning up, see, and then all sorts of guys, halfwits, like yourselves, with no experience, can go home like heroes for following a few fucking orders."

¶When later Napoleon is given the lousy job of sorting KIAC bags he saves some of the things that he finds for a bit of a laugh. He shoves them into his pockets, and later pulls them out for Teddy and Hill, while Teddy pounds a drum roll on his thigh.

"Oh, that's soft," Hill whines. "Din you get anything else?"

"Hold your horses," Napoleon says.

Other things Napoleon finds he shoves deeper into his pockets and only takes them out when he's alone at night in the shed where he sleeps now. These are mostly small posed photographs; girls around his own age, some clipped out of newspapers. Graduation announcements, yearbook photos. Others are studio quality; these he likes best. In which whole families are gathered. He has a whole collection of them, and looks at them sometimes and tries to pick out the dead boy.

He notices the way the families are configured, always in subtle but precise relation to each other: a standing hand on a sitting arm; a sitting arm on a kneeling shoulder. He comes to recognize the formula even and see the way that it's repeated, over and over, in the countless photographs that he lifts, over the weeks, from the bags.

¶They have given him unmistakable orders: it's only the

embarrassing articles, the porn, the dope, and any military souvenirs, that are to be removed. He sifts through the clothes, books, letters, tinned food and wrapped candy, and weeds out the girly magazines, the rubber gloves, the guns and the emptied Cong weapons. Once, he finds a wrapped-up thumb, and then in the same bag, a flat, greying ear. He buries them a little ways off and afterwards vomits over top of them, overflowing the shallow hole.

The photographs he takes as a small reward for his work, because no one is handing out tips. He takes: one photo from each bag, a handful of wrapped-up candy, and every second bag of dope he finds.

Later he shares these last items with the rest of the guys, but he never shares the photographs.

He keeps them with him in a deep inside pocket. He knows them: the contours of each connecting body part. The approximate length – for example – of the forearm of a boy in order that it touch the square waist of a girl. The width of a woman's shoulder in order that it be covered by a child's hand.

But sometimes Napoleon looks at the photographs and it's just parts. Just arms and waists and bald heads – disconnected from their neat clothes and shoes, and especially from their hard, brief smiles. Just bodies, then, touching, so subtly, in so strange a formula (a gutted hand over a shot-out shoulder, a slivered yellow moon of an ear resting there) that he thinks, *My God, what chance they should have fallen that way!*

Then his eyes and his mind refocus; the bodies and smiles and neat clothes return, as if just then rising in the emulsion, connecting the particulars to the whole.

The original family is restored to him, once more, complete. And he imagines himself as the youngest son. The toothless, grinning one, his arms thrown around the shoulders of a fat man.

2 "Now if you want to know how fucked up it was, think about Clark," my father said to me, on more than one occasion. "He was such a smart kid, dammit. What a waste." He shook his head and whistled out the words.

And though a little later he would talk to me long and enthusiastically about the adventures and misadventures that he and his buddies had had in Danang, everything that had to do with gambling and drinking, he never touched my original question that I had asked about Owen. Perhaps he didn't know.

Instead, when he spoke of Owen, he told me of the smallish fights they'd get into with each other, or with the other Marines; or the stories that Owen would tell as they burrowed at perpendicular angles into their foxholes at night; or how out to lunch they had felt after some especially good weed.

One time Hill (Arthur Hill was his name) called my father up on the phone; he told me about that. This was when my father was still living out in Fargo. "Geez, it was like being shot back in time," my father said, and he skimmed his hand across the tabletop. "Phwiiiiipp!" We were sitting inside at the kitchen table, where my father had made it out to a half-hearted meal, and his hand just nicked his beer a little as it shot along, so that the bottle turned in clunky circles on the pressed linoleum of the tabletop, and then came to rest, as if it had never been disturbed. "To hear that ol' Hill!" my father said to me in one of his really loud outright laughs. "What a guy! What a guy! He was better than the rest of them. Didn't want to be there: had an obsession with stock cars and really tall girls. He loved them really tall – he was a short little guy."

"Stock cars?"

"Yeah. I told him, Hill, if you get out of here you be sure to get yourself a nice little office somewhere, high up in the air. In Chicago – that's where he was from – somewhere where you don't have to go outside. A little cafeteria in there, a barber shop. So you know you wouldn't notice the weather. That's honestly what seemed would be the very best thing, the most you could ask out of life. There was a lot of shitty weather." He sucked on his cigarette. Sometimes he made a whistling noise when he breathed in sharp like that. The air just kind of all rushed in at once. "No more of this running around on the ground, no more of this blowing shit up, and you know what?"

My father looked up at me, his eyes bright. He was already coming up with a laugh. It was starting. "Ha – Haaa!" he said, before I could get out my own, "What?"

"The little fucker took my advice!" He stopped to cough a little but then went on. "He calls me up and he's in this big office building in Chicago, and he makes me guess where he is and of course I couldn't remember saying that exactly to Hill – not then. So I couldn't guess. I remembered when he said it though, so finally I just said, Come on Hill, I give up, just come out with it and tell me, man. I didn't want to say the wrong thing and make him feel bad, you know? Like maybe he was feeling happy, just thrilled to pieces that he finally got himself some walk-up in Detroit and here I'd be guessing a suburb in Miami ... that was the kind of guy Hill was, he could have gone any which way, and then he told me. Told me about the cafeteria, and how the place connected to the train and if he didn't want to he didn't have to go outside at all, only for the approximately seven seconds that it took him to run the half block of the street from the train to the lobby of his building, and I thought Jeeee-sus Christ! What the hell was I telling myself in those days? I should have been saying all that shit to me! I must have not been giving myself too many directions then. Nope," my father said. He had been speaking quickly, only pausing for brief intakes of breath, so he took a real breath then, and exhaled it slowly. "There wasn't a fucking thought in my head," he said. He held onto a bit of his hair with a balled-up fist, and gave his head a shake once or twice, from side to side, with his hand. "Yep, I was pretty well running on empty," he said, and tapped his forehead, and gave out another loud hoot that was at once a laugh and a cough, so that, combined, he didn't have to follow the one up with the other.

"Oh, but anyway," he said, realizing he'd derailed the story, "I said to Hill, You still wish you'd been a driver? and he said, Naaaaah! He said, I don't even watch that shit anymore, Ha! Ha! It's not permitted. The wife doesn't like it. Only thing I got is Andretti coasters for my beers, and that's it! I said, Good for you!"

"Did you ask him if his wife was tall?"

"You know, dammit," my father said, "I forgot about

that! I should have asked him! You little honey –" he said
to me, and then he repeated my question. "*Did you ask him
if his wife was tall.* I bet she's a squat little thing," he said. "I
can just see it – him having a real short wife." Then, "He'd
better!" he said, and slammed his beer on the table. "He'd
better!" he said again. "Can't have it all, the sonofabitch!"

3 The first thing that he does when he lands in Danang
is get a ride up north to find Clark. His stomach is
tight, and there's a strange feeling in his head. A light little
buzz. Not only because he's on his way to see Clark, probably, but because he hasn't slept in so long. Not at all on the
big commercial jet, on which, for most of the journey, he
flew. Not at all when they stopped to refuel; to get out, and
change planes, or sit around in the light of airport waiting
rooms. Not at all after shouldering his heavy bag to re-
board, this time a military plane, and fly again.

There are only one or two other enlisted guys on the
first plane, out of Indianapolis. They come around and feed
you orange juice if you want it, and kids draw in colouring
books, and cry. So, for the first time since the beginning
of his basic training, he feels like he's just himself, pretty
much alone. In uniform, he has found, he looks just like
anybody, and no one can tell. That during all that time out
in California there was something that set him apart, and
that was him thinking, it's only me that has this much
doubt in my gut. Or who feels this stupid. Or this afraid.

Sometimes even he couldn't tell the difference between
himself and the rest of them. He'd forget. About the dread,

about everything. Only to then have it hit him again, in a rush, like someone had punched him in the stomach and knocked the wind out of him.

But then on the airplane he doesn't feel afraid. He is pleased it's this nice commercial jet instead of the military plane, as if he is going on holiday like the other Americans. If he was going to leave at all, this was it: this was him doing it, and when he joined up, well, this – this exact feeling – was why.

It was Clark, actually, the reason he'd joined. Clark who'd slapped him on the back so hard that a bit of his breath really was knocked out of him and he had to gasp before he answered the question that Clark had asked him when he'd slammed him so hard. Making him feel again, with the hit, like the little kid brother, even though he was now taller than Clark and smoked more cigarettes.

"Why haven't you signed up, little brother?" Clark had said.

Being called 'little brother' of course didn't help. When he got his breath back he said to Clark, "I don't know." He kind of mumbled it. Clark hit him again, this time on the shoulder with a balled-up fist, "Well, get knowing," he said. "Look, there's nothing else going on here. Look at you. What are you wasting your time with now, anyway?"

Napoleon looked around him. They had been smoking a joint in their parents' garage. It had been going back and forth between them, but now it was stalled, Clark hanging onto it, waiting.

There was nothing in that garage but old cans of things, half emptied, and junked-up bikes. None of the bikes even worked any more. Both the boys took the second car downtown if they needed to go. Napoleon shrugged. "Nothing, I guess," he said.

After the joint, Napoleon would haul the garage door open and push the car out of it for Clark, at the wheel. Then, when the engine got going (Napoleon would have pushed the car halfway up the drive, but it was a short one) he'd jump in and Clark would gun it and they'd take off, zooming out of the drive, past the low houses of the residential street, and out to the highway.

"Fucking right!" Clark would yell. "You ready, my brother? You fucking ready for this?!"

Now, when this actually comes to pass, and the engine roars to life and Napoleon skips along next to the car for a jump or two before he manages to slide into place in the passenger's seat, and Clark says, "Fucking right!" there's a new note that Napoleon senses in his voice.

None of his friends joined up. Some of them have even talked about going to Canada. More usually, though, they just talk about moving around. Changing addresses will do the trick, usually, and it's not even that bad of a thing. It's pretty cool. Like *On The Road*.

But the biggest part of him just supposes that he won't get called. It seems impossible and a little silly to him to think they have his number.

¶So then, all of a sudden, he's on this plane. Being served orange juice. This kid with a colouring book crying sometimes in the seat in front of him.

He feels okay. But mostly that's because he's thinking about seeing Clark again, and kind of just showing off, like *Look, I got knowing*, having his brother give him that slap on the back again, only this time the breath wouldn't get knocked out of him, this time he'd slap him right back.

So that's what he does when he gets off the plane, and collects his luggage. He asks around. And whenever *he's* asked (once a big man comes over and says, *Son, what's your orders?* much more kindly then he would have expected), instead of saying, *Bravo company, First Battalion,* he says the name of Clark's unit, and it's that easy. He gets into the back of a truck with some other guys and pretty soon they're heading out of there. He feels good. That's it, he feels good. That (besides the tightness that he still feels in his gut) is what that light feeling has been inside his head all along.

The guys in the truck with him leave him alone. They're friends. Napoleon can tell that they've been here a while because they seem like they don't even notice anything, like the heat, or the smell. Like they don't have to watch everything like Napoleon does; his eyes wide, as though watching everything from inside a TV. Not the images, but just that feeling, the colour. Like being inside the screen. Everything bright like that, and fast.

There's some kids, he notices now, for example, that have been running, perhaps for some time already, beside them. And every time the truck slows, they clamber around it, and jump up and down along the side. By accident, Napoleon looks one of the kids in the eye.

The rest of the guys are yelling something, he notices now. Shouting back at the kids, who have been yelling, too – the same thing, over and over again – as they follow behind. "Chop Chop Chop Chop," Napoleon finally hears. "Chop, Chop, Chop," with their arms out, so – *oh,* he realizes, they're asking for something. *What do they want? A ride? Some money?* That's it, he thinks. Of course. Everybody wants money. And then it's funny to him that he could have been so dense and not notice that they were asking him for money before. He remembers with shame now how he just stared back at that boy, and didn't shrug, or make any move at all to show that he'd noticed anything.

But it turns out that it isn't money but food the kids want. The American guys, imitating them, say, "Chop Chop Chop," and pinch their noses, laughing. One of the guys rolls on the floor of the truck he's laughing so hard.

Napoleon wishes he could tell them to stop. Then he wishes he had a handful of American dollar bills. He would rain them down behind him if he could. He imagines himself with that much money, sending it behind him, in a storm.

Well, at least if they would stop it, it would be better. The tightness in his stomach is worse; it's not just his brother now.

And then one of the guys, the one that was laughing so hard, rolling around on the floor of the truck, finds a box full of C-rations. He chucks a can over the back of the truck and yells, "Here's your chop chop, you little assholes!" And as he does so the can narrowly misses another American guy's head, who says, "Hey, fuck – man, you almost took me out!" And is about to really get sore, but then thinks better of it. The other guy, the ringleader of the little group, hasn't noticed, and instead he picks up two of his own cans to throw. "I'll give you chop chop, you little motherfuck-ers!" he says, and whips the cans, both of them, one after the other, off the back of the truck.

The kids are screaming with delight. Running after the cans, which glint – each distinct and silver in the air before they fall. The one guy that almost got hit by the can and was angry for a minute is not angry anymore, and chucks a few. The laughing guy has gone back to laughing.

The kids fight over the cans behind them, and fall away. And then the fire goes out of the guys that are throwing the cans, and they lean back, calmer, and roll a few cigarettes. Napoleon is relieved. The kids continue to follow behind. They say, "Chop, Chop," now and then, but are ignored.

"Hey you want one, kid?" the angry guy says to Napoleon, extending a fatly rolled cigarette toward him. "You're awful quiet. He's awful quiet, ain't he?" he asks the ringleader. The ringleader, though, isn't interested in the amount of noise that Napoleon's making. He's smoking his cigarette as if he's never been more satisfied by anything in his life.

"Sure," says Napoleon, taking the cigarette from the angry guy. "Thanks, man. I appreciate it. Thanks." Then he hates himself for thanking the guy so much. One. One thank-you would have been enough.

¶They bump up a narrow road and stop in front of a huge, semi-round shed. It looks like a farm machinery shed, all made out of metal. It would be a machinery shed if this were another part of the world, if this had been a weekend trip from Des Moines that they'd been on instead. He startles himself in thinking suddenly of how this place is not-Des Moines. Of how he's dangling, his body at a weird angle from the earth, stuck out precariously on the other side of the world.

His blood, which had seemed to be rushing all into his head; no wonder about that.

"W'here, soldier" the laughing guy says, giving Napoleon a kick with his boot. Napoleon has to jump down out of the truck before this guy can get out. The others have leapt out over the sides, and are scattering now. But Napoleon, he just stands there, with no direction. The driver has banged out of the truck and he, too, is heading toward the low building, shouting something.

No one is, of course, expecting Napoleon. But somewhere there's Clark, Napoleon remembers. And with that his gut tightens again, and he heads toward the low building too.

¶He dropped a lot of acid when he was in high school, so when he walks into the building that's what he thinks is happening; his mind has been fucking disturbed, and here's the payoff. A great big German Shepherd dog, the head so large that it looks like the picture's all scrambled, who leaps at him, lashing itself against its chain. Somebody in the far corner of the room throws something at it. Napoleon can't see what it is that gets thrown, but whatever it is the dog doesn't notice at first either, and lunges again at Napoleon to the end of the chain. Then he gets lurched back, and falls and only then notices what it is that's been thrown. He picks up the object and starts licking away at it, his bright teeth showing, lips curled. It's dim in there, and Napoleon picks his way carefully, only a little forward, and then asks the first guy he sees. "Excuse me, sir – I'm looking for Haskell." His eyes haven't adjusted at this point, but when they do he realizes he didn't need to use that "sir." It's just a kid, no older than himself, and smaller. With pimples on his face.

The kid shouts, "Haskell?" and someone else asks – Napoleon thinks it's the bone-thrower – "Looking for Haskell? Officers' mess."

"Officers' mess," the kid repeats, turning.

"Hey," Napoleon says, "wait." He doesn't say "sir" this time. He just grabs at the kid's sleeve. "Aren't you going to tell me where the fuck the Officers' mess is?" He has noticed just how much bigger he is than the kid. Why the hell is everyone making him feel so small?

"Oh – yeah," the kid says, and he's embarrassed now in front of Napoleon. Or so Napoleon flatters himself. And then he gives him the directions to the mess. Napoleon has to keep reminding himself to pay attention; to listen to the kid. His mind wants to drift away from him, anywhere. He thinks now, for example, that this is the way it has to be – a question of attitude. That he can get through anything if he just remembers that. He should have said something to those jerks in the truck, even.

He'd have to work on that. Because there was no way he was going to survive here if he was just going to let any small asshole push him around. That feeling in the truck, for example. Then the disproportionate fear that he had felt when he first saw that dog. (Now curled up. Gnawing quietly on the bone). That would kill him before anything.

That's what he'd been doing for the last six months – his

basic training out in California – being pushed around. No wonder he hadn't felt like himself. That he had felt instead all loose and out of sorts, like he was only his shirt, without his body inside, being whipped around in a washing machine. But over here, man ... things felt different, it was like the fucking Wild West out here. There were no boundaries at all, no lines, or limits, but then of course, he's AWOL right now, he reminds himself. No wonder he feels this way.

He makes his way over to the Officers' mess. Every minute he expects to look up and see Clark there, with a big grin on, but he doesn't see him until he gets into the hall. Until he stands at the entrance, lets his eyes adjust and looks around. That's when he sees a long table about twenty yards back where four or five other guys are gathered, talking quietly.

He wishes that his brother would look up and see him and come over, like he's been expected. All of a sudden it seems too much for Napoleon, to walk over there himself, to open his mouth, to call out: "Clark!"

That sound would be like a crow calling if he let it out of his mouth right now.

An officer passes by him in the entrance. "You lookin' for somethin'?" he says. Napoleon shakes his head. "I'm sorry," he says. Then nods in Clark's direction. "My brother –" he says. And the officer (not too much older than Napoleon) says, "You Haskell's brother?"

He's got an old face, though, the officer. The kind of face where you can tell exactly just what kind of middle-aged man he'll be. (Balding, a little tired, but nonetheless pleasant looking. Professorial. The kind of bald man ladies like.) Napoleon nods and then he grins, even though he doesn't want to.

"Ohhh! Oh yeah!?" The professor guy says, "Well, nice to meet you." He sticks out his hand, which Napoleon takes, and as he's shaking it the professor waves with his other hand over to the table where Clark's sitting. "Hey, Haskell," he says, "your brother's here."

Clark looks up then, toward the professor, and toward Napoleon, both of whom are still standing, facing one another with their hands clasped. Napoleon sees Clark's face and how at first it's incredulous, and then it's pleased. He does, he really does look pleased. But first, before that, there's a surprise like he thinks his eyes are playing tricks on him. But then his brain adjusts and takes it all in: the professor and his kid brother, who last he heard was still in basic training out in California, and then he gets up from the table and strolls over to meet them. Napoleon just stands there, waiting.

When Clark gets within an arm's length, he stretches out his hand toward Napoleon and Napoleon grasps it in both of his. "Hey, buddy," Clark says.

"Hi!" says Napoleon.

Then, after what seems like a very long time they sit down. Someone has gone to get both of them a beer. Napoleon tells Clark some things, but he tells them all out of order. About his training. Leaving out how much he hated it. Everything about it – the base, the entire State of California. About the last time he saw their parents. Leaving out how his mother had clung to him and wet his shirt and said, I wish you were a university man. How she'd then looked angrily at his father who was standing like a post in his too-big jacket with the collar standing up so that it acted like a shield to the wind and obscured part of his face. How she'd said to him, why couldn't I have raised two university men? How his father had reached out and tugged at her arm, tugged her away from him, a little more fiercely than was nice. A little more fiercely, to be fair, than he probably had wanted to tug her away. How Napoleon was unable to see if his father was really angry or not because his face was mostly shielded by the high collar. But then how, when his father did approach, he could see that his face was set into a tight line that, if it tended toward anything, tended toward cheer. How he extended his hand to his son, and how Napoleon had taken it, but limply, and then, after thinking for a moment, how the father had taken up the son very briefly in his arms in an attempt at an embrace. One that fell, however, so short of intimacy that for Napoleon the gesture rather emphasized instead of bridged the divide. "Don't get yourself into any trouble," his father had said, and turned away, taking his mother with him.

It doesn't take them long to finish the beer. And it doesn't give Napoleon much to talk about, leaving all that stuff out. Clark doesn't seem to have a lot to say either. It's hot, and both of them seem thirsty. Clark just nods and nods again, as Napoleon speaks, and then he introduces him to the few men that are sitting around them at the table, and then he stands up, his beer drained. Napoleon stands up too after a few seconds. Clark stretches his hand out over the table and takes Napoleon's up in his. The table is too fat to have second thoughts and close the handshake in an embrace. Instead, Clark bangs the side of Napoleon's shoulder with his other, flat and open, hand. "Well, soldier," he says, "I guess you'd better get back to your unit."

Napoleon thinks everybody is looking at them. He feels uncomfortable. Then confused. Like he's forgotten things. He looks around for his bag. "Oh, well, fuck, okay, I'm out," he says, giving his shoulders a shrug.

Then he gives his brother as firm a shake and a squeeze on the hand as he can, and turns and walks the hell out of there.

¶It's not too hard to find a ride back to Danang, and then he gets into the right vehicle and heads to his unit. He tries to feel good, and brave, like he did on the plane or like he did when he told that kid not to walk away from him, but instead he feels mostly sick to his stomach now. The beer started it, then maybe the drive. He feels nauseous and cramped up, like he hasn't shit for a year. Also, his tiredness seems to crash down all around him suddenly. He has a splitting headache.

The following of orders is some comfort now. No one requires anything of him, after all, except for the movement of his body from one place to another, and he is still, if vaguely, capable of that.

"Wait over there," a man tells him and Napoleon gets his body up and walks it over into a corner of a low building which is not unlike the low metal building he'd been in earlier in the day.

As an experiment, he tries to pick the body's foot up, and does so. Then he puts it down.

¶He is issued a rifle, and puts his name in red tape on the butt of it in the way that he is told. Then somehow he finds a way to ask for a bathroom. They tell him just wait, but he says he really can't wait anymore, and he's told to wait again. He shrugs, but is worried. He goes back to the butt of the rifle, smoothing his name. Finally someone shows him to an outdoor privy and he goes in there and sits down on the hot seat and lets his bowels go and it's such a relief that he cries too, because he forgets which part of him he's supposed to be letting go. He gets them all mixed up together, and then he realizes what a mess he is, sitting there, shitting and crying, and he hits his hand on his head several times as hard as he can and says, "Fuck you, fuck you, fuck you," and then realizes that the kid (just another enlisted guy like himself) who showed him to the privy is still standing outside the door, which is thin, waiting to take him back again. He's embarrassed in remembering that, and finishes up as quickly as he can.

When he comes out, he doesn't say anything to the other guy and just follows him back inside.

¶He finds, then, that they're standing in a row, and he is side by side with all the rest of the new guys, and there's a big old Gunny coming down the line, and then he's nearer and nearer, saying, "Who's Haskell?" His name sounds very deep and mean. Damn, he thinks, and doesn't answer for a minute. But then he realizes that that's not going to work: he's just smeared his name onto the butt of his gun.

"Who's Haskell?" The gunnery sergeant barks out again, and so he admits it. He steps out of the line, and salutes. "Haskell, sir," he says.

"You," the Gunny says. "Sergeant Bright asks you to report. Roberts here'll take you." Napoleon has a whole pile of freshly issued gear beside him, but they say don't worry about that, and he's not really worried about that, so he leaves and just follows this other guy inside again. His stomach cramps. Also he's thinking, *Damn damn damn. I'm fucking caught now. I'm fucking in for it now.*

"You Haskell?" this Sergeant says to Napoleon.

"Yes, sir," says Napoleon.

"Relation to Clark Haskell, right?"

"Yes, sir," Napoleon says, "Clark's my brother, sir."

The Sergeant belts out a short laugh and comes out from around the desk to slap Napoleon on the shoulder. "I'm pleased," he says. "You can tell your brother that. Pleased to have you in my unit." He pauses. "Well, I'll be damned," he says, and takes a close look at Napoleon. "Yep," he says, "I see it. See the familial resemblance. You as fine a man as your brother?" Pause. "What?"

"Well, I don't know, sir," Napoleon says.

He gets another slap on the arm. "Let's try that again," the Sergeant says. "You as fine a man as your brother?"

He's not really mad, though. At least Napoleon doesn't think he is.

"Uh —" the Sergeant doesn't give him enough time, though, and jumps in. "The answer," he says, "as for almost everything, is *Yes, sir.*"

"Yes, sir," Napoleon says.

"Well, good," the Sergeant says back. Then he chuckles and moves back behind his desk. He lays his big flat hands on the big flat desk, and leans back in his bendable chair. "Never met a finer officer, myself," he says, "as that particular Haskell: your brother." Again he pauses, looking off into the space of the room, as if actually that other Haskell's presence is more real to the Sergeant in that moment than the Haskell which has recalled him to mind. The one who's actually there, really present, swaying a little, and attempting to concentrate on what is happening to him, and what the Sergeant is saying, and how he should be acting toward him.

"I look forward," the Sergeant says finally, "to seeing the same kind of man in you. I'm sure you have a lot in common." He looks up at Napoleon with these words. He looks up at him quite kindly, and smiles.

"I hope I won't disappoint you, sir," Napoleon says. And that starts the man up again. He leans back further in his bendable chair, in a caricature of repose, and it must be a funny story that he's telling because his eyes are all lit up and grinning, his big teeth showing. He's a handsome man. He has light, arched eyebrows and very clear, fair skin, like a boy's. Though now, around his eyes and mouth, it has articulated itself as finally quite separate from his features, creasing into a spray of small, independent lines. The pronouncement of his square chin gives his face an added air of authority. Napoleon wishes he had a chin like that one, and maybe because he wishes this he misses all but the tail end of the Sergeant's story. His nod, he hopes, is sufficient enough reply.

Something about a bet – a gentleman's agreement – and then the Sergeant says, bringing things to a close, "and never in my life, never in all my life, have I known a man to throw a grenade so far."

The encounter is over after that, and Napoleon is led

back to the yard, after a firm handshake from the Sergeant. The yard has been vacated now. Napoleon picks up all of his recently issued gear, but can't get a real good method down of holding it all. It seems awkward, and things keep slipping around as he walks. He has to keep asking the soldier, who leads him to the barracks that he's been assigned, to stop because of this, and in those moments he shifts the positions of the things in his hands.

4 One day my father accompanied me out in Henry's boat. I went ahead of him, down to the dock, and he walked, very slowly, behind. Every ten or twelve steps he would pause to breathe, his chin tucked in close to his chest. In one hand, he held onto two beers.

When he arrived, and had settled himself into the bow of the boat, I drove very fast so that the engine would roar. In truth, I was disappointed that my father had come along.

We drove past the island with the disappearing road, and out behind it into a small cove dotted with cottages. I slowed the boat for some people who were out in sea-kayaks, and they waved at us as we approached. There were some people set up at the campsite in that cove too. They had a big tent up, and a tarp over the picnic table, and a motorboat out on the water with a bunch of rods sticking out of the back like the spines on a fish.

"Why don't you tell me a story," my father said.

"I don't know," I said. "I don't think I can think of any."

"Sure you can," my father said. "Just think of one thing, tell me one thing."

But instead of complying with my father's request, I asked: "So, was that where you met Owen?" Preferring, I guess, to be installed – more comfortably – in the past.

"Hey," my father said. "What about that story?"

I shrugged, and didn't answer. My father, too, was silent for a while. Then, shifting to a lower and more careful tone, he said, very quietly: "Why do you want to know about all of this anyway?"

He seemed not to expect a reply, though, and I was grateful to him for that, and after a while it was he who spoke again, saying, "Because, you know you don't have to worry about any of this shit, thank Christ. If there's one thing I'm grateful for –" But then his voice broke off again. "Oh, Honey –" he said. And for once he did not reach out, to touch me, as he said those words.

There was something in his voice, though – an apology for something too big for him, and which was perhaps not even intended for me – and still, he regarded me as he spoke. Still, it was as though he were in fact reaching out. As though he were in fact touching me. But for once he did not, and after some time passed into which we again said nothing, I started the motor on the boat and drove on.

¶Later, skidding by shore – near to where I'd drifted alone, at the bottom of Henry's boat, in a previous afternoon – I said, "It's around here."

"What's around here, Honeybunch?" my father said. He was once again in a jovial mood.

"Henry's house," I said. "His old one. We pass over it every time we're on this lake. Do you ever think about that?"

"Oh, yeah, I guess I think about that," my father said. "And those old ghosts of Owen's sometimes."

"You don't believe in ghosts," I told him.

My father grinned. "I do more than I believe in most things," he said. Then he took out a cigarette and fooled around in his shirt pocket for a lighter. "But no," he said, "I don't. I just think about them anyway sometimes." Then there was another long pause. The boat rocked a little from side to side on a passing wake. "Actually, I don't think Owen believed in them either, it was just something to talk about," my father said. "Just some silly thing that reminded him of home. He loved this place. That was one thing we knew."

He gave the cigarette a few puffs and then chucked it into the bottom of the boat, where it absorbed water.

¶Later still, my father asked: "What happens to ghosts in water? Can they swim? Are they made up of water, in that case, instead of air?" He trailed his fingers, then free of the cigarette, in the lake. "Could I be touching one right now?" he said, looking at his water hand, his eyes twinkling at me, "As well as right now?" And he wriggled the fingers of the arm still wrapped in its sling.

"I don't know," I said. I wanted to get home quickly now, so I tried to start the engine, but it sputtered and stuck.

"So, what about you?" my father asked, not giving up. "Do you believe in them?"

"No," I said.

"Well, you did!" he told me. "You *sure did*!" And reminded me of all the nights I had come screaming in from the government house yard, after Helen had leapt at me as though from nowhere, on the path.

"Hey," I said. "If you can wonder about the material nature of a ghost when you don't believe in them, I can be afraid of them when I don't believe in them."

"I was just wondering what people who did believe in them thought."

"Sure," I said. "No. I just think it's a nice spooky sort of way that people have to pretend that things, that people, don't just, you know – go."

"Yup," my father said. "That sounds right."

I gave the engine another tug, and it sputtered, but this time with greater promise. Then it roared itself to life. "So what were you always screaming about when you were a kid, then?" my father yelled.

Actually he had started the sentence out just talking in a normal tone, in the near silence. But when the engine roared he'd had to yell. He finished the sentence out – himself nearly screaming. I just shrugged at him across the boat, exaggeratedly, in reply. Then I turned the boat around, pointing it back to Henry's dock.

There was no use talking now, with the engine on.

¶That evening Gerry called from Fargo. He couldn't come in August, he said, like he'd planned, but would try for October instead.

My father shook his head, and gave my shoulder a half-hearted squeeze.

"I can last till spring," he told me. "October is still plenty of time."

But by seven o clock that night, with the mixture of beer

and pills in his head, my father was nearly catatonic on the couch, and Henry departed to his bedroom, without TV. I went upstairs too and left my father alone.

The next morning he could not get out of bed, and all the liquor had been emptied from the house.

"I have a cold," my father said. He looked like hell. I warmed up some soup at noon, but he wouldn't touch it. "Take it away," he growled at me.

Toward mid-afternoon, I told him I was going to the store and did he need anything?

"A priest," my father said.

"You're Protestant," I told him, "and you don't believe in God."

"That was dumb of me," my father said. "That was cocky. I shouldn't have been so cocky. Don't you be so cocky," he said.

He didn't drink at all that day, and it was very quiet in the house. But then, the next day, he got up saying that he was feeling much better.

"Wow!" he told me. "I really felt like death. Now I know how it feels, anyway. It's bad," he said. "It's worse than I thought."

In the early afternoon we drove to Massena and picked up my father's prescription. "It's the alcohol. I can't drink it like I used to," my father complained. But on our way back, still on the American side, he stopped at the liquor exchange and got a couple more bottles of something. I didn't go inside. And I didn't say anything when he got back to the truck, and so we drove in silence, until my father said, "What? You don't want to hear any stories?"

"Not really," I said.

"No?" He seemed mean. "Got any for me?"

I ignored him, but then he told me one anyway, even though I hadn't wanted one, or asked.

"So, one time," my father said.

5 The four of them are in Danang, and Teddy says, "Let's really rip it up tonight." They're getting antsy as hell. They drink steadily for most of the evening and then they smoke a joint. It's the fattest one they've ever seen, and for a while they just pass it around, unlit. It's Owen who rolls. "That's craftsmanship," Napoleon tells him.

"We're gonna be sitting on another planet," Teddy says. A little fiercely.

They don't watch each other this time, but let each man hang on for as long as he likes, and hold his breath for whatever duration. Sometimes they splutter and cough out the smoke. It's embarrassing if they choke hard.

There's a certain curiosity tonight: each thinking about what Teddy had said. About how high it might be possible to get. If it might be a measurable distance from the place that they are.

Napoleon has the same feeling for a moment as when he first arrived in the country. When he was, for all intents and purposes, AWOL. And so he tells the other guys about that as the joint gets smoked down to a little more than half its size. Everyone laughs out loud really hard. Napoleon laughs so hard that it occurs to him that he may not be able to stop. But the prospect is, in itself, so funny, that it makes him laugh even harder. What if it really does stick? They'd send him home, for sure. They'd have to. Imagine. Discharged for medical reasons. *Incessant laughter, sir. Unstoppable, it seems*, the doctor would say, sticking a popsicle stick in his mouth, which would already be open, on account of him laughing so hard. *Nope. This boy's not fit to fight*.

Wouldn't be bad. No — think of it — it would be great! Only then he guesses it might be a *dishonourable discharge*. Laughing. That would be a bummer. Would it? He loses the thought. What would be dishonourable? Dis — honour. The word presupposes a certain thing.

Much later Napoleon gets up and walks very slowly back to his bunk. He holds onto the wall sometimes, in the pitch-dark, like he's scaling a cliff. Sometimes he holds so tightly onto the rough cement that later he will notice that the tips of his fingers are raw, and wonder why. He looks for cracks that might prove a firm hold, then he finds his bunk and lies down.

He is so happy to be lying down — to have, against all odds, travelled the great distance of the room and come to rest now, in just this way — that he wants to account for himself somehow. The way that he is — each small part, seemingly so disparate — in some way, a singular, moveable body; resting, but alive. The way that he's been blown that way, as accidental as a star; by chance, by some cataclysmic, unreckonable force, greater than himself. The way that he has perhaps already long ago been extinguished — so that his own thoughts are in fact only an echo of someone else's, or his own. The way that he, scattered into a thousand, inchoate, diffusive directions ... he, a singular thing, a particle – a part-icular – body, still hurtling itself objectively through space and time, has yet, by accident, come to rest somehow, briefly, now. His feet, for example. Resting only a short distance apart from one another, and yet taking up two entirely different sections of the bed. Or rather not taking up: displacing, in fact, *no bed at all*. Think of it! To have displaced objectively nothing, his whole life! To have simply hurtled through – an impenetrable, impenetrating thing. The feet, for example. The legs, the knees …

But then suddenly that's all there is. Just that: the knees. And then again: the knees, the knees. He can go no further. There is no sensation any longer, no knees at all that he can find, but only this repetition, this stutter of a noise in his head.

Is this then – the final diminishing? The last echo of thought in his head? The whole world shakes now. Stutters, and pounds.

If it is, he never would have picked it for himself. He wouldn't have dreamed it up even if he'd had another hundred billion years. Interesting that it will be like that, when it comes. If now. If ever. Nothing you could ever see coming. Even if you lay in your own bed for a hundred years, just waiting. Even if you counted out the seconds, the semi-seconds, of its passing, pausing at each wearisome metronomic tick, saying, *now*, then *now*, then *now*, it would still somehow occur in the middle of everything: between the revolution of one millisecond and another, a surprise, even then.

Still, it is not so bad, and he remains. Perhaps that is all it ever is. To just, finally, give up on the progression, the constant click-clicking forward. To pause, to stay put, to be remained of yourself; to *become* that remaining.

¶ "Well, what was it?" I asked. Because he just left me there, that way. Just broke off then, at what seemed to be halfway through the story. Left himself, lying in that bed, thinking *well if this is the end* …

"We were under mortar attack," my father said. "I would have figured it out if I'd have had any of my wits about me."

"What should you have done?"

"Oh, I don't know, I guess climbed under the bed or something, shit my pants, I don't know. There wasn't anything that I could have done right then much different than I did. I was happy in the morning when I figured it all out. Then we went somewhere else."

"Where'd you go?"

"I don't know. I really can't remember the name of anything. Danang, but that's about it. Maybe if I looked at a map or something, but I really don't think even that would help. I don't think I ever really knew where we were. They never told us, or anything. It was just up, down. We got our orders, climbed into planes, choppers, got into the backs of trucks – and then we got out. We did what we were told, it was all the same fucking country. We didn't care. It wasn't like sightseeing or anything."

"I know that," I said.

"It just didn't mean anything to us, is all," my father said. "Where we were. We just got dropped off and that was it, that was Vietnam. There we were – and you'd know it, too. Clumsy! Jesus! You knew where we were!" He took

134

a sip off his cigarette. "Johnson got piped in once, and he says, Viet Cong can sit in a hole for a couple of days with nothing to eat and drink, where our boys can't go twenty minutes without wanting a smoke and a cup of coffee ..." My father stuttered out the words in imitation of the static of a radio. "It was like any government work that way," he said. He gave a short bark of a laugh. Then, "Well, no. Not quite. I don't know, Honey," he said, and turned to look at me for the first time in a while. He'd been talking out the window. "I'm a poor — I'm a poor source," he said. "I've a real poor memory for the place." He paused again and then said quickly, as if with the next sentence he wished to get rid of the thing entirely, "Imagine absolute fucking chaos, then that's it, you got it." When I didn't say anything, he continued. "Honestly, I think you'd be better off watching the movies. Brando. In *Apocalypse Now*, for instance."

I thought he was joking, and I gave a short laugh. "What?" I said.

"Yeah," my father agreed, "just like that. Insanity. My stories are all *and then, and then, and then,* when it didn't happen like that to me." He breathed in, "Yep," he said. In the way Henry did, nearly swallowing the word. "You might hear a name," he said, "but you didn't have a map. We were just like elephants, crashing around. Elephants, working for the government. Wanting coffee and smokes."

¶That night my father beat Henry and I soundly in a game of euchre, which we played three-handed. Then, just before he clicked out the kitchen light and made his way to bed, saying, "Well, that's it for me, folks. I'm turning in," he reached again into his secret store of poetry and song lyrics and movie quotations that he kept at the back of his brain and, laying his hands one on top of the other, he lifted his head dramatically, and closed his eyes.

"Remember me when I am dead," my father said, "and simplify me when I'm dead."

He paused, then asked us, beaming: "Who said that? Where did that come from?" He'd opened his eyes again, and began looking back and forth between Henry and I, enthusiastically, as if we were contestants and he was the game-show host.

"Sounds like poetry," Henry said.

I nodded agreement. "The words of a rank sentimentalist," I said. But I liked it. It made me feel happy and sad at the same time. And also like maybe everything was not such a big mystery after all.

"Yeah," my father could have said to me, then, following my lead: "Why?" So that I could say back to him: "Why do you interfere with my little romances?"

He always remembered better than me.

But that time my father let the Bogart reference slide, and it drifted away like the words of the poem that he had remembered, which had come from nowhere.

There was no score on the ball game between the Red Sox and the Orioles. Henry turned it off and reached for a chunk of newspaper to read from my father's pile until the second game of the night came on.

My father scratched a dozen or so more words into his crossword, one right after the other, suddenly inspired. Then he lay down his pen and clicked off the light, saying that to us about "turning in."

Very soon afterward I also made my way to bed, leaving Henry alone to watch the late-night game on TV.

6 Napoleon is never certain when he becomes aware of *what's next*; of when one moment ceases to be itself and becomes another. Has he been wandering around in circles this whole time, or has he been sitting? And if sitting, how sitting? Propped up by some object?

But at some point it happens. There is a point at which he knows.

Some of the guys are shouting now, or swearing, or shaking their fists. Bean is there too. But he is no more formidable now, nor less, than any of the other men. Involuntarily, Napoleon covers his ears. But really, it can't be much noise. If he pays attention he can count them. One. Two. Three. Four at the most. He looks around for Owen. For Hill, for Teddy. But he doesn't see them. It's been half a day now since they've been milling around. Since the chopper came, went. Since these orders, which are not orders. Which are just a low buzz, a sort of racket in his brain. Once, Napoleon is nudged in the boot by a big guy named Mike who has always to Napoleon resembled a very thin bear. He's got a great big head, and sad, slow eyes. Now, he nudges Napoleon, touching Napoleon's boot with his own. The contact causes Napoleon to wince in pain. His feet are the fucking sorest in the world.

"We're going back?" Mike asks. His big bear eyes move, watery. Unfixed in his head.

"That's the command."

Napoleon's voice is sour in his mouth. He comes across mean and that's a surprise because he doesn't feel mean. Another question is asked, but Napoleon doesn't hear it, and only shakes his head at the bear, imitating the bear's own gentle side to side.

¶It only seems like more because he can't decide any longer who's who, and because they are making so much noise.

The ones that aren't making noise, like he and the bear, are just standing or sitting around like dumb-asses.

A guy named Pike is one. He's a small guy who really looks like a fish, with a squished-up mouth and buggy eyes. That's not why they call him Pike, though. That really is his name.

The other guy is Looch. A big Italian. It turns out (one time Napoleon caught a glimpse of the guy's red tape on the end of his gun) that Looch is short for Luciano or something. He was surprised when he saw that, to think that guy had a real name too.

The last guy's a lieutenant they call Tiny, but really he's a great big motherfucker. From Jersey. An Irish with the real name Francie. Always talking about that. Being from Jersey and an Irish, and a great big motherfucker to boot. It's these guys that are making most of the noise, and at first Napoleon's unable to actually see Lieutenant Bean; he just knows he must be there. But then he does see him, and without knowing what he's doing, or why, Napoleon gets up and walks over to him, and says something, which even to himself he cannot identify.

No one either agrees or disagrees with whatever it is that Napoleon has said, or what Bean has then said in reply. And then they go.

Napoleon goes. His feet hurt more than ever.

¶On the outskirts of the village they come across a small hooch, and as the squad approaches they can see three or four women crowded under its low awning. One of the women is holding a child, and there are about five or six more children crowded behind. Their heads appear and then disappear at revolving angles, in the low and heavily shadowed region at the back of the hooch. Their eyes, when they do appear, are very large in their heads, like they must see things twice over.

Everything seems like that. As though it has already happened. As though it has already frozen itself into the shape that it had, and now will continue to hold.

¶But then with a jolt – an actual physical jolt, as Bean pushes past him to enter the hooch – Napoleon realizes that the thing is alive and moving toward some end. That he is part of the thing. That he may in fact be the thing. He feels sick to his stomach, but only in the way that he has felt all along, since he arrived here, off the passenger plane. Only now he knows what the sickness has been.

And there he'd been, thinking of his feet, for Christ's sake. And now Bean inside the hooch. Bean hitting the women on their backsides with the butt of his gun. Bean taking the baby from the mother's arms. That cry. That single note.

The butt of his gun where his name, like theirs, must be emblazoned in red.

Or, Napoleon wonders. Might that be a privilege of rank? An anonymous gun?

The women leap up at the touch of the gun, and out of the hooch, so that they stand in front of it now, in the grass. The children, too, come out of hiding, exposed, and stand as though at great distances from one another. It is like he is looking at everything the wrong way round, through the butt end of a telescope. Everything turned inside out now, and upside down. Christ, Christ, Napoleon thinks, and again a voice appears in his throat, but again he cannot make out what it says, or what Bean has replied. He only notices the way that Bean has started to sweat — in patterns — through his shirt.

Tiny's like a horse at the gate. The women stand barefoot in the grass. Napoleon doesn't want to look at their faces, but then he does.

The Lieutenant has by now made a small but precise mark on the young woman's arm, where he grabbed her in the place where the baby had been, and steered her into a small clearing, adjacent to the path. Bean lifts his gun but finds that it has already been fired, so he puts it down.

The shots have rung out, yes, but in the past tense. The moment erased somehow.

And then Owen. A long, infinitesimal second later. Owen, charging, his own gun askew in his outstretched hand. Then another shot rings out. This time in the present tense. As if in slow motion. So for a long time afterwards, there is just that — single — final note. And Owen. Falling. Owen — continuing to fall.

In that moment, Napoleon feels such a strong and physical desire to follow that same course that it is as if by instinct that he moves toward Owen. That he too begins to fall. But then, abruptly, he receives a kick in his side, and Tiny is there, dragging him up from the ground. He realizes – with the impact of the boot, which his body has stalled – his own relative stillness. He gets up, no longer recognizing Owen.

In a high-pitched voice Bean says: "That motherfucker would have killed me," but Napoleon is uncertain who Bean is referring to. He sees him wet his lips. "Alright," Bean says, looking directly at Napoleon now. "Not the kids. But everything else," and although Napoleon is again uncertain of the meaning, or the object of what Bean has said, he feels also a tremendous relief, to which the words seem in some way to correspond.

They move. Tiny and Looch carry the dead man, and the kids remain, making that sound. A high, ringing note.

¶They set the village on fire.

Once, as they are moving through it, half of it burning, Napoleon bumps into Hill. Hill has his head down. He says, "Watch it."

Napoleon hasn't seen Teddy anywhere, but he must have seen him, just without realizing it was Teddy he'd seen.

And where is Hill?

And where is Owen, now?

¶A matter of minutes. Half of an hour at most.

For a third time that day they move over that ground. Away from the village, where there is no village now, and past the hooch, the last one to be burned. Napoleon doesn't wonder about the children, who are nowhere to be seen. He is only happy that they're gone.

Tiny and Looch carry the dead man, which makes the return journey slow.

¶Several days pass. Napoleon doesn't talk to anyone, and no one talks to him; not Teddy, not Hill.

He thinks about shooting himself in the leg. He thinks about that all the time. When would be the best time to do it? At night? During a march, making it appear accidental?

Should he perhaps do it now?

Should he do it now?

Because he could. He could do it. But *how* do it? What part of the leg would be safest for the hit, without being, perhaps, *too safe?*

He could pull his gun out now. He could shoot himself now.

Then, on maybe the fourth day (the second day since they've returned to the base), he goes to the chaplain. "Father, something is wrong. I don't feel right."

The chaplain is a young guy, nice enough.

"Sit down," and Napoleon looks around him for a chair and sits down in the one that squeaks.

The chaplain speaks as though into balloons, which float up, empty, and disconnected from anything. It's raining. It is always fucking raining. Then Napoleon starts to cry and says "*Do* something, *dammit!*" and even lays his hand briefly on the chaplain's white shoulder. Then he quickly removes it. And realizes he's sworn. "You've got to do something."

Quieter, by way of apology.

¶That's how he ends up in the KIAC shed, sorting those bags. For a while the squad sticks around, so he still sees Teddy and Hill and that's when he gathers what he does, and shares it with them. They get high, and look at porn together, and Hill complains, and each day Napoleon collects a few more photographs. But pretty soon Teddy and Hill stop coming because they say it's too dangerous to let the other guys see them with Napoleon. They shrug their shoulders and say *sorry.*

"You're screwed, man," Teddy tells him. "You watch your back. I'm serious."

"Shit," Napoleon says. "I know."

At night he sleeps with his rifle, so that when he wakes up the shape of it is marked on his side.

The last time he sees them, Teddy says: "Why the fucking chaplain, man? That guy's a prick."

"I don't know," Napoleon says, and passes a thin half-smoked joint to Hill. "I don't know. Who the fuck else?"

"That was a real dickhead move," Teddy says. "You should have talked to me first. You should have listened to me."

"Oh yeah?" Napoleon says, and for a moment he wishes he could feel angry at being spoken to like that, by Teddy, who is his friend. But then he thinks that's funny: to still think of people that way. Of the way they were or were not supposed to act toward you, or anyone else. Friends, or not friends.

Fuck that. Plus, he doesn't have the energy to be angry, or care.

"Oh yeah?" Napoleon says. "What would you have suggested?"

"I would've told you to keep your fucking mouth shut," Teddy says. "If you want my opinion, Owen was looking for trouble, and now so are you."

"Yeah, well – too bad," Napoleon says.

"Yeah. Too bad."

The joint has gone out. It's on Hill again. He sucks on it and there's a little sip, a popping sound as the burnt-out end bit gets pulled back into the butt of the joint, and goes out. There's not enough in there to light it up again so Hill just holds it, very delicately between his two fingers, even though in a moment he will just get up and squash it in the mud.

"Well, you got yourself into some real trouble now," Teddy says. Again. "I don't envy you that. It's just lucky for you you're not coming out with us again. Guys don't see things the way you do. They say you really coloured things up."

He looks at Napoleon briefly, then shrugs, and raises his hands as if to say, "I can't help you now." But the gesture is silly. Everyone knows it, and no one is blaming him. There's nothing that Teddy can do.

¶Only a short time later, there's a court hearing in which Napoleon testifies. One time, just before he is escorted by another officer to the stand, Napoleon passes Bean in the hall.

"You really fucked up, soldier," Bean says. "You really fucked up."

Napoleon is only happy that Bean doesn't mention his brother. Maybe he doesn't know about Clark. About how far Clark can throw a grenade. But he doesn't care about that. He would just rather not have his brother mentioned.

In the extremity of it, in fact, his not caring, Napoleon is startled by the prospect of never caring for anything again.

This is somewhat a relief. It will be an easier life than the one he's expected.

¶During this time he tries not to think at all. Not about Owen. Not about anything. And every time his mind wanders to that threshold, teasingly close to the door, he pulls it back into a far corner, and sits it blankly down again. It's true. He wants the hell out; wants it so bad, like he's never wanted anything. It's not even a feeling he wants it so bad. Even when he's up there on the stand, answering those questions, he's not listening to his own voice, but instead thinking, could I say something *so bad?* Could they send me home if I did?

He wonders what it would take, but somehow is compelled (in the same way that he was compelled to keep his gun from his leg) to answer the questions correctly; to be polite. To nod, sit down, to leave the stand when asked.

And when he thinks of being sent home it's not to a place he imagines being sent. He does not picture his mother or his father, welcoming him. There are no socks, no corridors, no arms folding. He doesn't imagine the one or two girls he might like to have greet him, if he could. Or think about his mother's kitchen, or his bed. He doesn't imagine the town, the theatre, the park, the car – all those things that over the months he's been away he's recreated so vividly in his mind. No. He just imagines *not being here.* That's it. There is no place on earth that he thinks of to replace it.

¶Sometimes, though, he thinks of Owen's boat, and that is the closest he comes to thinking about Owen. How they had promised it to one another, semi-buried in foxholes one night, in an interminable rain. How the boat got mixed up with all the other stories that Owen would tell, and which Napoleon more frequently requested – about his mother's and grandmother's ghosts – because of the way they made him laugh, and made Owen's eyes light up even if he couldn't see them, half teasing, half mean, saying, "You don't fucking believe me?" But also because of the way that, when Owen spoke of them, they became – no longer make-believe spectres of some other, imaginary, world – real and physical companions, in the way that his own mother did, when he imagined her in the heat, padding toward him down an invisible hall.

On several occasions, Owen has carefully described the principle of it to Napoleon, drawing diagrams in the mud, so that he might better understand. The way the volume of water displaced at both the stern and the bow of the boat, for example, should correspond equally to the weight of the waves on the hull, in order that it absorb the resulting pressure of its own momentum; the small hills and holes in the water, that is, which *the vessel itself has caused*.

No, there is no place that Napoleon imagines for himself, and even the boat is not a boat, and not even an idea, now. Just as Owen is no longer Owen, and even his ghosts are, if there could be such a thing, non-ghosts, now. And there are. That's it. He's surrounded by them. Non-ghosts, non-thoughts, non-words, non-people. Even himself. Now less the sum of his parts. Yes, it seems, in fact, that there are more of these empty spaces in the world than there are things with which to fill them. More things that are not than that are. No wonder that the cracks show. Yes. There are too many empty spaces in the world, and he is one of them.

¶On one of his last days out in the field, just before he would meet the chaplain, they come across a dead man. A little NVA guy, his head collapsed but his body still firm: bloated up, making him appear larger than he would have been alive.

Pike says: "Hey, check it out. I could use those boots," and he bends down and unties them. They can't get jungle-boots, and some of the guys are worse off than others in the big clodhoppers they wear because their feet are too small – like Pike's – to fit into any of the more decent pairs.

The dead man's boots don't fit either. "This guy has big fucking feet," Pike says. "Those can't have fit him." Then, because Pike's passed them over, the other guys all line up and try the boots on. They're not nice boots, but they're better than the ones they have and, anyway, a change. All their own boots are out, around them, they look like dead birds. And everyone's messed-up feet are out, aired for a minute, waiting for a turn. Napoleon's feet are, it turns out, no worse than anyone's. They are, all of them, bloody and white, with fungus and stuff that looks rotten. He's surprised about that, about how his are no worse when he'd thought his were the worst in the world. That there they had been, marching along, together, all of them with the very worst feet in the world.

The boots fit Napoleon and because they have to keep going, they say, "Fine. Haskell wears them, but we'll switch

147

off. Looch, you can be next, man," and they keep going until Napoleon realizes with a sick jerk in his belly that he's wearing a dead man's shoes.

He takes off the boots and walks on without them. He thinks with an almost amused surprise when he takes them off, "Fuck, what do I need these for!" Then he re-wraps his blisters in the rags that he'd covered them in before and keeps going, and he feels better without the dead man's shoes.

Later, of course, everyone is angry. He shouldn't have lost those boots. He looks back on the moment that he took them off and (although disgust still rises in him at the thought of them) he's able to see their point.

Pike tells Napoleon that Looch wants to flatten him. Pike says he'll see what he can do to hold him off. He lowers his voice and says to Napoleon, "I know it's not your fault. I know you're crazy now."

That's nice of him, but Pike says he's not promising anything.

¶So Teddy and Hill say they can't see Napoleon anymore, and pretty soon the squad moves on anyway. They come one more time. "See you," Napoleon says. "Don't get fucking killed." Then he continues to sort through the bags and sleep with his gun until they put him on another squad.

On another assignment, with new guys, whose names he doesn't ever learn.

He doesn't collect the porn or the candy in that in-between time, after Hill and Teddy don't come to see him anymore. Sometimes he collects the weed, and then he smokes it and lies in among all those bags, when he's supposed to be working, and takes the photographs out of his inside pocket and looks at them for a while.

Then he realizes he's let his guard down and let too much time slip by and he gets up in a hurry and tears through the bags one after the other, through all the dead-guy things. Missing stuff, no doubt, because he goes through them so quickly.

But he thinks: If some mother or wife (in Delaware, Washington State, wherever) should come across some porn, or some dope, in her son's or her husband's bag — *If that's what it comes down to her knowing*, well. That'll be some comfort, or should be. That is what Napoleon thinks.

Then he's put on another assignment and gets shot in the leg. He didn't even have to do it himself, but now he wishes he had. He wishes he'd put his own bullet through. But thinks, anyway, that he must be very powerful, because he wished so hard, and then it came.

¶He lies in the hospital for two weeks and doesn't think. Or else he thinks but he thinks about nothing, about the way that everything is white.

The sheets, especially. He loves the way the sheets are white.

He spends some time, too, wishing he were dying. He thinks he's powerful enough that if he thinks about dying for enough time then he might die too. But he doesn't. He keeps living, instead. He looks at those white sheets and he lives.

He does keep wishing, though. He wishes because if

this is his dying, then this whiteness constitutes his end. He can think of nothing more lovely than that; than an end so white.

He's on so many drugs, that's why. He knows that. They come and give them to him, and he looks forward to their coming. He likes the way the drugs make him feel; it's better than anything. A clean feeling, a wide open, anything feeling, like he felt when he was AWOL, only this time much better because now the feeling is not being pushed forward, shuttled. Through circumstances of the past into circumstances of the future. It just is, self-contained, and outside of everything, and if it had a colour guess what colour it would be?

Then abruptly one day they say he's better, and after that they send him home.

7 "It was the weather that was the worst," my father told me. "Sometimes, you'd be on duty, camped out all night, and you just had to sit," he said, "and sit and sit. And watch. And what the fuck we were watching for half the time I didn't know. Or –" after thinking a moment he added – "or what the fuck I would do, I didn't know, but there I was …" He leaned forward in his chair to hug his knees, and let his jaw fall slack, "Sitting there, and then it would rain, you know … They'd just say, You're here. And then that would be you for the night. Just a steady drizzle all night," my father said. "It rained all fucking night, and I was cold, Honey, Jesus, my teeth were chattering away in my head, all fucking night long. I hated that sound."

A change had come into my father's voice then. So

that it was as though, in those moments, he was no longer speaking to me at all, or even to himself. As though he were speaking, instead, into someone else's story, at some distance from his own, that had nothing to do with him, or with me, and over which he had very little control.

It's strange. To speak to your father, like that: when he doesn't know that he's your father. When it happened, as often it did, particularly at the end, it always made me want to shake him, as though he was sleeping. Interrupt him somehow. But instead I always stayed even more still than usual at those times, perhaps even holding my breath. So far was I removed from him, then, and therefore also from myself, that it seemed I hardly existed at all.

¶It was a surprise to all of us when Helen arrived at the end of August – having left Sophia with my mother in Orono. She stayed for three days and during that time it was as though we traversed again – as on that interminable drive east from Fargo – an endless and unfamiliar terrain, this time of our own creation. We felt not the claustrophobia of my father's truck, then, but its opposite. As though we inhabited separate and remote corners of his illimitable and still-coveted prairie. As though all things had been levelled; emptied off. As though – if indeed we had thought to send them out – our shouts would have rung nearly soundlessly in our own ears, swallowed up by the unconquerable landscape between us.

¶On the second day, Helen and I went out to Henry's garage, behind the government house, and stared together at my father's boat, where it still rested on the haphazard blocks where Henry and I had raised it. "Well," Helen said. "It isn't much, is it?" And by her tone, which did not seem to address the boat, or anything in particular, I could not tell what she meant, and did not ask.

¶Then, just before her departure, after leaving Henry at the dock, Helen wandered again up to the house, where my father – with a beer in one hand and a crossword in the other – and I had remained. But even after she had said goodbye, first to one of us, and then the other, she did not go, but lingered instead, and in that time we regarded one another and no one spoke. Then she turned, and started toward the drive.

It was not until then, until the actual turn, that my father called out. So that, again, Helen paused. And again, for the last time, we three regarded one another. My father at one end of the porch, me at another, and Helen, hovering, already half-turned on the stair.

"Oh," my father had called out simply. As though Helen's final, decisive, step – the moment finally sprung from its hold – had initiated in him an equal and correlative action of his own, and that with that sudden forward burst, into the incontrovertible now that the turn indicated, my father had lurched, equally, in a different direction. Attempting, if not to resist, than at least to pause everything for a little while; unwilling as he was, finally, to give way to the ultimate upsetting of a balance which would have us all very soon dropping away, unmoored, into a future even more imaginary than the past.

And that note – of apology, of alarm – that had rung out

in my father's voice at that moment, in that final "Oh!" as Helen turned, I recognized to be the same note that had rung out in his voice not long before, when he had questioned me as to my motivation for desiring to know something of him, and of the war. As if he actually did believe that stories were things that you could disassemble, into isolate, removable parts, and hold certain parts closer, and certain parts further away. And that, having always been careful to dismantle himself from the story he had hoped to be ours, he was sorry for the way that he had let himself sometimes slip, despite his best intentions, quietly into our lives. Sorry for the way that he had allowed – without intending it, and in ways he had not anticipated – our world to be the same world that he also inhabited.

"It's just –" my father explained to Helen as she turned, "you looked a little unhappy there, my little Honey." As though unhappiness was in fact a foreign and an unaccountable thing, unfamiliar to our family – whose presence, within the limits of our lives, he could neither explain nor understand.

"Oh, no," Helen said. "No, no." And then she did go.

Because, in the end, my mother and father had done exactly what they'd hoped that they might, it was not exactly unhappiness that I felt then, either. Instead, I felt only very strange and small. Like I was sitting inside myself in little pieces. As though I could, if I wished, take myself apart like a Russian doll and find myself in layers there, each one smaller, and more hollowed than the last. Until, at the very bottom, and for want only of tools precise enough with which to do so, I could go no further.

We sat out on the porch for some time after Helen

had gone, not speaking. Then my father went back to his puzzle.

Every now and then he would look up and ask, "Honey – you'd know this. What's the capital of …?" Or, "You'd know this. Who wrote …?"

But I never did know.

¶Then, in the last days of August, while rummaging for a lost prescription in a kitchen drawer, where, for a generation and a half, receipts, old letters, photographs and paperwork had been indiscriminately piled, my father stumbled across a poem that I had written for Henry in the tenth grade.

When I came back from the lake that evening he was waiting for me, poem in hand, evidently pleased with his find, and before I was even properly in the door, he was already reading it out loud in the deep contralto he reserved for recitations.

In the poem, Henry is a simple, happy man; just the way that I had imagined him as a child, when he had existed as though for me alone; a side character even to his own story. I had summarized him as though in a single gesticulation; in one of the eloquent, but cursory waves of my father's hand, say, which – though always used to some effect – never really indicated anything at all.

It seemed remarkable to me, then, as I listened to my father, that I had at any time imagined it all so simply; that Henry could have been for me, just, a man who fished. Who fixed the engines on boats. Who solved math problems with beatific patience in the evenings. As though in the calculation of things – the requisite addition and subtraction; the anticipated and final division – there had been, and would be, no remainder. That it could turn out to be, after all (as he perhaps had hoped all along, no less than I), a perfectly balanced equation, the answer to which he had already known.

It seemed, after all, that I'd expected, instead of too much, too little from life. But my father, his eyes shining, was untroubled, and lingered – ignorant to my derisive shouts of laughter – on the poem's last note.

"I think," my father said when he was done – a little defensively – "that it's a nice little poem."

I gave another loud shout of what I'd intended to be a laugh, but by a strange alchemy it was converted to a sob inside my throat, so that I had to pause and swallow several times, quite hard.

"I don't want," I explained to my father, finally, biting each word, "to have written a 'nice little poem.'"

My father, who had not noticed the change in my voice, only shrugged his one movable shoulder, and, with his working hand, gave a characteristic wave. "So," he said. "Write another. But don't be too sad. Be like Whitman. I like it when you're like Whitman. He always made the most of everything."

¶Having returned the poem to its place on top of the still unsorted paper files, my father moved out to the porch. He walked slowly, very straight and tall, as though there were pieces inside of him that were made out of glass. Then, having arrived finally at his destination, he cleared his throat loudly, leaned heavily on the porch rail, and lit a cigarette.

I remained where I was. In the kitchen. I drew my knees to my chest, and put my head in my hands, but I did not cry. I kept my eyes wide open so I would not, and because of that I could see precisely the lines my hands made against the floor, where they didn't join. The triangle of light that formed. A brown half-moon, a yellow square. I stared for so long there, at those irreconcilable shapes on the floor, and did not listen so intently to the noises of that house: to my father's deliberate inhales, his stuttered coughs, the deep throat-clearings of the porch, outside, that I didn't even notice when Henry arrived.

Henry himself. How would I have known him?

It was as though – gliding swiftly and unseen – he had become a ghost in his own house, and so was only just suddenly there beside me saying, "Look!" And when I did look, taking my hands away from my eyes, which I had not closed, I saw that his hands were cupped in front of me where my own had been.

Then he opened them and a bird flew out.

Henry, with a small laugh of alarm, looked down at his hands in bleak surprise, as though he had not guessed what they'd contained. Then my father was there at the door, leaning in from the porch with just his cigarette outside – choosing, for the first time, to remember that he wasn't allowed to smoke in the house.

"What the –" my father started to say.

Henry pointed to the corner behind the open door. He seemed embarrassed. "I found it over there," he said. "I didn't mean to let it go just then. I just wanted," he turned to look at me with a shrug, "to show you –" But then the bird made a sudden dive toward our feet and he left off, giving another loud whoop and a holler as it rose again, to the ceiling.

My father took charge. "Stand by the windows!" he shouted at us. But Henry and I remained where we were, motionless.

"What —" this time Henry began.

"The windows!" my father said. And so we moved. Henry to the near window, and I to the one on the opposite wall.

My father, having now illegally entered the room, began to wave the burning end of his cigarette at the bird. He danced awkwardly, going first one way, and then the other, but the bird seemed to anticipate his every step, mirroring each swoop, each lunge, each one-handed wave that my father's cigarette made in the air.

Finally, though — as if it had always known where the open door had been and had, with every loop, every seemingly mistaken angle of his flight, tended toward it all along — the bird simply flew away.

We followed him out onto the porch. Watched him as he disappeared around the side of the hedge. Then Henry leaned back in his chair and laughed, and my father laughed too.

Finally, so did I.

But then, when we were quiet again, my father said: "You know what that means, don't you? A bird?" He paused. "It means," he said, and his eyes twinkled, "a death in the house." I suppose he had meant it as a bit of a joke but Henry ignored him, and declared only, in admonishment to both my father and I, "We'll do better to keep the door closed now."

"Anyway," I said, addressing my father's remark instead of Henry's, and rolling my eyes. "I know you don't believe in that sort of thing."

My father winked at me. "I don't believe in a lot of true things," he said. "A lot of stuff just happens, you know, my little Honey, whether I personally believe in it or not."

That night, just before he fell into his trance, my father again read aloud my tenth-grade poem, this time to Henry. I tried not to listen. And then, because that was impossible, I tried not to mind. Then, because that too proved impossible, I thought instead of that fragment of the poem my father had recited to us once, not long before: "Simplify me when I'm dead."

For some reason I always remembered it after my father had said it. It just stuck in my head.

8 On my last afternoon at the government house I took my father for a long drive out on the back roads between Long Sault and Ingleside. My father kept his beer goosenecked at his feet, snapping them as we drove, one after another, from their hold, and emptying them all afternoon – so that, by the time we had driven an hour, he'd relaxed into comfortable, semi-conscious repose. He reclined in his seat, his head tilted back to the late afternoon sun, closing his eyes sometimes, but not because he seemed tired.

No. On the contrary. All afternoon he remained attentive, vigilant as a hawk, even with his eyes closed; anticipating the stop signs, as always, while they were still miles away.

Hours later, still not ready to return, I drove the car right past the government house, stopping at the end of the lake road, and we sat out there for some time, looking back to where the lake stretched behind us in three directions. The thin wedge of Henry's dock was just barely visible to us there.

Then we drove back the way that we came. But, just before we slid again into the government house drive, completing the return, my father turned to me and said: "I'm writing a poem too, you know. I'm basing it on that photograph that I like so much. Of you and Sophia."

It was the photograph that Helen had sent to my father two years before; the one he had kept on the windowsill of his old Fargo place, and had spent such a long time looking at when in the dead of winter his pipes had frozen and he'd stood at the sink to melt his snow.

He still kept it with him at the government house. Not pasted up on the wall, or framed, or even on the refrigerator door where he might more frequently see it, but in amongst the clutter of his bedside table instead: his beer caps, used handkerchiefs, pill bottles, and twists of chewing tobacco that he spat out like an owl.

"When it's done," my father said, "I'll send it to you to proof. It's my very first poem."

"That's wonderful," I said. We had by then pulled up in front of the government house but neither of us moved to get out of the car.

"I can be like Whitman too, you know," my father said. "I can see beauty in things." He looked at me. "When it has to do with my sweethearts, I sure can." He gave my shoulder an almost authentic-seeming squeeze. All the while his eyes shining, in that way that they did sometimes. Like underwater lights, searching for something.

Also, though, he was just goofing around.

But then a few days later, he called my mother's house in Orono where finally I'd returned, and read me what he'd written over the phone. For the first time in a long time, then, it felt uncomplicated. It was just love, after all, that I felt for my father, and that wasn't so hard.

"It's not Whitman yet," my father informed me. "But it's something."

¶Later that same day, he called again and read the poem out loud a second time.

"What did you change?" I asked.

My father sighed.

The end-stop in the middle, he told me, was a comma now so that the two sections of the poem were joined in a single sentence.

"Oh, yeah," I said. "Okay. I like it."

"I think it makes a difference," he said. "Don't you?"

"Yeah," I said.

"You couldn't tell." He was disappointed.

"Not at first," I said. "But I can now. I think it's good."

"Whitman would have noticed," my father said.

¶Then, in the early part of November, as though in speaking of the war my father had opened a seam through which the rest of the world now burst, he received a telephone call from a historian at Indiana State. His name was George Parada. For almost three years, he had been researching the incident at Quang Tri – which my father had described to me for the first time during that summer.

"I had a hard time tracking you down," Parada told my father when he called. "The records indicate that you live in Fargo, North Dakota."

"Tell me about it," my father replied.

Parada had been a member of the same division as my father. He'd worked as the battalion mail clerk from early 1967 until the end of the war – and so, though he had no first-hand experience of the incident in question, the rumours of its consequences had not escaped him.

He lived in Terre Haute now, a professor at the university there, and had begun to compile accounts of the incident, Operation Liberty II, as it had been known, in response to the erroneous account published some time after the war by ex-marine Frank Higgins. Higgins had, according to Parada, so exaggerated the scale of the operation, that he numbered the dead at three hundred, making the incident appear to be a miniature My-Lai. He hoped that his own book would uncover the truth of the incident, and lay to rest, finally, Higgins' false testimony – which threatened, he said, to turn the whole thing into noise.

It was tough going, though, because there was not much to either prove or disprove Higgins' account, and for months – though he sorted endlessly through military records, and transcribed interviews – Parada was left with no obvious results. Speaking to two of the government counsel lawyers, when finally he located them, had yielded next to nothing. Michael Baird and Peter Francie had refused to speak at all. "Oh that old thing again," Francie had said before he'd hung up the phone. "That thing with Haskell. The guy was a nut. Nothing happened that night. SOP the whole way." Robert Pike didn't "remember shit about anything."

Among Parada's personal acquaintances he had had even less notable success. They, too, either declined to speak of the event, or were unlocatable. Two of them – and Teddy (Edward Fairly) turned out to be one – had committed suicide; Teddy having hanged himself off a second-floor balcony in Hood River, Washington, sometime in the early eighties.

All that was left for Parada to work with was contained in the forty-year-old transcript of the trial: a five-hundred-page document, which he had managed to get hold of in its entirety. The existence of this document was also a revelation for my father when he spoke to Parada of it in the weeks before his death. He had always assumed that his hearing had been a small and embarrassingly personal affair, and was unaware that anyone, besides himself, had testified.

It turned out that my father's apparently futile visit to the chaplain had in fact sparked an investigation that had lasted two and a half years. In the end, though, for lack of real evidence, and due to the subjective nature of the witness's testimonies, the case against Bean and the other commanding officers of the implicated patrols was eventually thrown out.

Unfortunately for Parada, when he was finally able to get in touch with my father, he too was of little help. By that time he had already shifted into noticeable confusion. In fact, Parada's telephone call was one of the earliest indicators that this was the case. Although less than three months before my father had spoken unfalteringly to me about the incident in question, never hesitating in point of fact (as though the words that he would use had already been written, and had sat for years, spooled on his tongue), by the time of his conversations with Parada he was no longer able to clearly recall the events of the twenty-second of October at all, or of the trial that ensued.

A short time later it became evident that not only the remote past had disappeared for my father: My own recent visit to the government house had as well. Stumbling slightly in humble accusation over the phone, my father insisted that I hardly visited him at all. It made me sad then, and it still does, to think of it. And also not a little afraid. To think that despite our best intentions we may, in the end – and necessarily – leave the people that we love quite extraordinarily alone.

¶After his initial conversation with Parada, my father's confusion grew rapidly, and a second telephone call, which followed only six days after the first, left him, long afterwards, repeating fragments of the conversation to himself in utter bewilderment. Sometimes just a single word, for hours.

Later, it would be objects instead of words that confounded him: he would throw up his hands in frustration and rage when observing, for example, within arm's reach, a scrap of tissue on the bedside table, a disc of chewing tobacco, or the cordless telephone. "What the fuck does this have to do with anything?" he would shout at each object in turn. As though it were the items themselves, and not the circumstances which had arranged them there, that had become for him unidentifiable.

When Parada phoned for a third and final time, and, later that same afternoon I asked my father about it, he said only: "You know, I had a dream last night where I met everyone at once, in strange circumstances, and then I woke up."

It was during this last conversation, though, of which Parada told me more later on, that my father seemed able to recollect again, and quite plainly, the events at Quang Tri. But instead of answering any of Parada's questions himself, he threw them back at Parada – only then to interrupt any attempted reply with an objection or a shout: "No!" he would say. "That wasn't the way that it happened at all!"

But – uselessly for Parada – this was a response evoked equally by Higgins' version of the events as by Parada's own. Though he was pressed to continue with his own version of things, my father, by that time, would or could not. And so Parada – having reached the end of what had at one time been a long list of possible purveyors – at last admitted to having failed in his pursuit.

¶Ten days later, my father died. Henry telephoned the ambulance and they telephoned the police. For six hours – while my father remained on his bed in the opposite room, stretched in a final convex image of himself, and of repose – Henry was interrogated by two RCMP officers who drank bucketfuls of coffee in the government house kitchen and examined my father's collection of photographs, prescriptions and disorderly files, curious to know why he had come to die so far away from home.

When, finally, they closed their books and took my father away, it was only Henry who was left, all alone, in the government house. There were not even any ghosts that night. He went outside, and, with his strong arms, in a few short pumps, wheeled himself down to the edge of the dock, where he sat for several hours.

Epilogue

¶In early January of the following year, I received a package in the mail, forwarded from Henry to my new address in Portland, where I had found a job with the *Maine Sunday Telegram*. The package was from George Parada, who we had not thought to inform of my father's death. It included the thirty-page transcript of my father's testimony.

Parada and I spoke several times on the telephone after that, and I told him what little I knew of my father's experiences from the bits and pieces I had gathered over the course of our last summer together at the government house.

The information was, however – except on a personal level – of little use to Parada; the Higgins' account had been, by then, effectively discredited, and though it was true that Parada had once hoped to replace the account with the true story of what had happened that night, he seemed, at the point at which I spoke to him, at last content to accept the fact that the events were irresolvable – relegated as they had been to the memories and imaginations of men who were, for their various reasons, and to greater or lesser extents, now unspeaking. To accept, that is, that the actions of war, being part of that great and ancient chain of command capable of establishing an event, even at the moment of its occurrence, as though it was already deeply in the past, were such that it would be impossible, and rather unsportsmanlike, to expound.

But if this truly was the case, then what difference did it make if Higgins had expressed the deaths of one or two as the deaths of three hundred? No. There were certainly distinctions that needed to be made. It was just a matter of how, and by whom.

When, in the winter following my father's death, I read the transcript of his testimony — most of which I will now record below — my own sense of these things was only further confounded, and sometimes now I'm astonished by the audacity of any attempt, including my own, at understanding anything at all. But then I think about my father again, and about how, in the closing remarks of his cross-examination, when he was warned: "These are very serious proceedings, you know, and generalities can be very dangerous," he replied, unshaken: "Well, sir, I've only answered the questions that have been asked to the best of my ability."

And so, in these pages, I have also tried to record what I know to be true; the truth, anyway, as it exists at this, my own particular intersection of it; at this singular and otherwise obscure point along its complicated and transitional course. As it pauses here, I mean, almost imperceptibly, and for only so long, before continuing on, in its uncountable directions.

I think now that that's really the most — the best — we can do: answer the questions that pose themselves to us, and describe, if only to ourselves, the things that we have loved, and believed in, and the actions that we have or would have liked to have taken, and will take now, and do take, over and over again, in the quiet parts of our minds.

But really, I find it hard to imagine any method at all of understanding the events of the twenty-second of October, 1967. Or of the way that afterwards they repeated themselves, and continue to repeat themselves: in same or in variant forms, charting again their recurrent course. Among those who (long after the events themselves had shuttled into other moments, and other lives; disguising themselves in divergent sadnesses, misunderstandings, expectations and desires) witness them still. And among those who, like my mother and Helen and Henry and me, were not aware of them at all, but likewise witnessed, and continue to witness them. Who likewise still hope to uncover, recognize, and subsequently comprehend their otherwise inexplicable presence in our lives.

DIRECT EXAMINATION
Questions by Captain Harding

Q: State your full name and rank.
A: Napoleon Edward Haskell.

Q: What was your first name?
A: Napoleon.

Q: Your organization, please?
A: B and S company, 1/1.

Q: Your armed force, please?
A: United States Marine Corps.

Q: Were you a member of "Bravo" company, 1/1, on or about 21 and 22 October, 1967?
A: Yes, sir, I was.

Q: Do you know Lieutenant BEAN?
A: Yes, sir.

Q: Would you point to him, please?
A: Right there, sir.

GC: Let the record so indicate.

Q: Where were you on the evening of 21 October 1967?
A: We were on Operation Liberty II, sir.

Q: And where was this?

A: West of the air strip in South Dong Ha.

Q: What was the mission out there as far as you knew?

A: I thought it was to locate possible enemy mortar positions.

Q: Was there an incident sometime on the night of 21 October or the early morning of 22 October when someone was injured?

A: Yes, sir, there was.

Q: Would you please tell us what happened?

A: ADAMSEN, sir?

Q: Yes, go ahead.

A: We had just passed through, and were veering away from this little ville, and we turned up on this hillside. Our platoon was the point platoon. Just as we got to the top of the hill a mine was detonated. ADAMSEN was killed, and KLINE and CAREY were wounded, sir.

Q: That was your platoon, which platoon?

A: First platoon.

Q: And who was the first platoon commander at that time?

A: Lieutenant FRANCIE, sir.

Q: Do you know where Lieutenant FRANCIE was in relation to Lance Corporal ADAMSEN when the mine went off?

A: I believe he was right in front of him, sir.

Q: Did you see Lieutenant FRANCIE there?

A: I know he was somewhere directly in front of me, FRANCIE was in front of CAREY, CAREY was directly in front of me. I believe Lieutenant FRANCIE was right in front of ADAMSEN.

Q: Was this the order you had been in shortly before the accident took place?

A: Yes, sir.

Q: What did you do when this booby trap went off?

A: I just got down, sir, and placed the machine gun to the left flank.

Q: You were with the machine gun?

A: Yes, sir.

Q: What was your position with the machine gun?

A: Ammo operator.

Q: Who else was in your machine gun team?

A: I believe I was carrying the gun, sir.

Q: Who else was in your machine gun team?

A: LUCIANO and HILL, sir.

Q: What was the next thing that you remember doing?

A: Next they were calling some of the men up to carry the wounded and the dead man down to be medevaced.

Q: How long did the medevac process take?

A: From the time the booby trap went off to the time the chopper lifted off, probably a half hour or so.

Q: Did you find out, or did you know of, what type of booby trap this was?
A: No, sir.

Q: You never did see it?
A: No, sir.

Q: Did you hear anyone say what it was?
A: Some people were saying it probably was a ChiCon, and I heard someone say it might have been command detonated.

Q: Did your machine gun prep fire the LZ before the helicopters came?
A: No, sir.

Q: Were you aware of any prep firing going on?
A: Yes, I believe there was prep firing going on.

Q: Did you witness any sniper rounds coming into your position?
A: Not to my knowledge, sir.

Q: Approximately what time did this device go off?
A: I couldn't really say, sir, it may have been twelve.

Q: This was 2400 or thereabouts?
A: Yes, sir.

Q: What was the lighting like around the spot where you were at the time?

A: It wasn't too bad. You could distinguish who somebody was.

Q: Do you remember whether there was any moon?

A: No, I don't.

Q: Did there come a time when your platoon or your machine gun team was to move out of that position?

A: Yes, sir, they did.

Q: And what let you know that you were going to move out?

A: I just got the word that the first platoon was going to move back to the ville, sir.

Q: Do you remember from whom you got this word?

A: Not really, sir. I just heard people talking.

Q: Did you hear anything else besides the fact that you were going to go out?

A: Yes, sir. They said that we were going to kill everyone in the ville and burn it down.

Q: I'd like you to think back and see if you can tell this investigation who it was that told you this.

A: I believe that it was Lieutenant FRANCIE.

Q: Are you reasonably sure that it was FRANCIE that told you this?

A: Yes, reasonably, sir.

Q: Did anyone else say anything about the patrol to you?
A: Not that I could tell you, sir. It was just generally what I figured was happening.

Q: What was FRANCIE's attitude when he told you this? Was it just another patrol to him, or did he seem particularly enthused, or what?
A: FRANCIE was always saying, "get some," or something like that.

Q: What did you interpret this to mean?
A: Just a slang expression of his. That was what I thought his attitude was.

Q: What was he going to go out and get, some cotton, or what?
A: I just thought that he thought this was the right thing to do, that we should go out and do this.

Q: How would you express the same idea that he expressed to you in your words?
A: Just that he thought this was the right thing to do.

Q: What was the right thing to do?
A: To go out and burn the ville and kill the people.

Q: Was this your interpretation?
A: Yes, sir.

Q: His expression, "get some," was that what you thought it meant?

A: Loosely, sir, yes.

Q: Think back and give us, as nearly as you can remember, what FRANCIE told you at that time, his exact words as near as you can.

A: I don't believe I could do it, sir. I'm not even terribly certain it was FRANCIE that said it.

Q: Was it your impression then that someone talked to you and said you were going out in the ville to "get some," or to kill everything?

A: Yes, sir.

Q: Was anything less than that said?

A: Like that it might just be a routine patrol?

Q: Right.

A: It may have been, sir, I'm not certain.

Q: Were you present for any patrol briefing?

A: No, sir.

Q: Do you know who gave the patrol order for your platoon to your particular patrol?

A: No, sir, I don't.

Q: What was the next thing you did after someone came up and told you that you were going to go out and kill what was in the ville?

A: We were still milling around the area there, and it wasn't long until we – we took our packs off before we went out. We just got together and went.

Q: Did you hear anything else said from the time that the booby trap went off until this particular incident you just mentioned as to what was to be done with the ville – to the ville?

A: I suppose I heard some conversation about it, but I can't tell you what was said.

Q: Was there anything that struck you as unusual about the patrol that you were getting ready to go out on?

A: Yes, sir, I thought it unusual that I hadn't ever been on a patrol where civilians were intentionally supposed to be killed.

Q: Did you have this impression before going on the patrol?

A: Yes.

Q: Can you trace that impression down to anyone other than the possibility of FRANCIE?

A: No, sir.

Q: Could you help us out with anything else in that area?

A: No, sir.

Q: As far as you know then, you got this idea from one individual that came up and told you about this, is that right?

A: No, sir, I knew about it before FRANCIE told me about it. That is the first instance I can remember anybody telling me about it, but at that time I knew we were going out.

Q: Had you spoken with Sergeant BRIGHT before this time?
A: No, sir.

Q: Had you spoken with Lieutenant BEAN?
A: I don't believe so, sir.

Q: Would you say this idea you had did not come directly from any of those individuals I just mentioned?
A: No, sir.

Q: Did you have any knowledge, or were you told what the source of the word was that you were going to kill civilians?
A: I assumed it had come from "Bravo 6," sir, because Lieutenant FRANCIE wouldn't just up and take his platoon out without any higher word.

Q: Is this purely an assumption on your part? Was there anything said to you that would help you conclude this?
A: After we got out on patrol, I believe it was Lieutenant BEAN that said to Sergeant BRIGHT that the word from "Bravo 6" was to kill all the people and burn all the hooches.

Q: Aside from — now did you hear BEAN say this yourself?
A: Yes, sir.

Q: Aside from what you heard BEAN say, was there any other relationship in your own mind at that time, not assumptions, was there any factual connection between this word to go out and kill and "Bravo 6"?

A: No, sir, there wasn't.

Q: Was there any other word about what was to be done in this ville?

A: No, sir.

Q: At any other time aside from the incident, did Lieutenant BEAN hear anything about what the mission of the patrol was?

A: What do you mean by that?

Q: At any other time did you hear what the mission of the patrol was?

A: Not to my recollection, sir.

Q: Where did you go when you left the LZ with your machine gun?

A: It's pretty hard to tell exactly. We moved out of the LZ, which was a field out over this ditch. There was a little bamboo bridge that we crossed. We just moved out on the trail.

Q: What were the elements of the patrol?

A: As far as I know, it was what was left of the second and the third squads.

Q: Do you remember any names of the individuals that were on the patrol?

A: There were – from weapons there were FRANCIE, HILL, LUCIANO, and myself, Sergeant BRISCOE was there, Sergeant BRIGHT, Lieutenant BEAN, FAIRLY, DOC NEUMANN.

Q: What was your machine gun team's position in this patrol as you moved out?

A: We must have been in the second squad because I remember Sergeant BRISCOE in front of me about a couple of men.

Q: Do you know who was in front of him?

A: I'm not really sure. I believe HILL and LUCIANO were in front of me.

Q: Did any incidents occur on your patrol?

A: Yes, sir.

Q: What was the first incident that occurred?

A: It wasn't really much. We had these bunkers along the side of the trail, one or two man bunkers.

Q: Could you see bunkers along the patrol route?

A: You could see the holes leading into the ground.

Q: Did you see any fighting holes in the trail?

A: I guess there were fighting holes.

Q: What happened next?

A: We kept moving. We prepped the treeline with our

machine gun. We crossed over into the treeline from this
trail, we just kept moving for a while. We moved across
this open field and there was a hooch right on the other
side of the open field there back of the trees a little ways.
There was a little treeline along the trail and the hooch
was off to the right of the side.

Q: What happened at the hooch?
A: They sent in a couple of men to burn it.

Q: Did you see any men go up to burn it?
A: Yes, sir, I saw them go in there.

Q: Do you know who they were?
A: No, sir, I don't.

Q: Please continue.
A: They said there was a bunch of people in there.

Q: Did you hear somebody say that, was the word passed to
you, or what?
A: I guess I heard someone say it, sir.

Q: You didn't see the people at the time?
A: No, they were evidently inside the bunker.

Q: I want you to tell me what you heard and saw, not what
you assumed or anything else. What did you see next?
A: They got the people outside, out of the hooch.

Q: Did you see them bring the people out?

A: The door of the hooch was facing the same way I was.

Q: You saw some people come out?
A: I saw some people gathered on the inside of the house.

Q: Who was in that group of people?
A: It was pretty hard to tell from that distance, sir, I wasn't too acquainted with them.

Q: What did you do next?
A: We set up our machine gun right at the mouth, so to speak, of this path that led into the hooch.

Q: What was the mission of your machine gun there?
A: I don't know. It was to have a place for security.

Q: Who told you to put your machine gun there?
A: I don't know, I guess we just set it down there.

Q: Up to this point, did you hear any word about what was going on?
A: No, sir.

Q: Did you hear any grenades go off?
A: At the first part of the patrol, yes, sir.

Q: Did you hear any grenades go off in the area of the hooch?
A: No, sir.

Q: Did anyone tell you what was going on up at the front part of the squad?

A: There wasn't really a front part of the squad at that time, sir. We were bunched up on this large trail we were on, with the exception of the people that had gone into the hooch. I could see as well as anyone what was happening.

Q: Did people actually go inside the hooch?

A: Up to the hooch, sir.

Q: You said you could see what was happening. What was happening?

A: The people just got them outside. The next thing I remember was that Sergeant BRIGHT told BEAN that he couldn't kill any kids.

Q: Did you know what prompted this statement on the part of Sergeant BRIGHT?

A: I can't remember what it was.

Q: What did Sergeant BRIGHT say?

A: He just told BEAN that he couldn't kill any kids.

Q: Did Sergeant BRIGHT say anything else?

A: No, sir.

Q: Was anything else said at that time?

A: That's when BEAN said there was an order, sir.

Q: What was it that BEAN said at that time?

A: I believe that he said that "Bravo 6" had given the order that all people in the village were to be killed, that the village was to be burned down.

Q: Did he say this to Sergeant BRIGHT's face?
A: He had come back. He was standing on the smaller path leading to the hooch, sir. Sergeant BRIGHT was somewhere on the main trail.

Q: Can you tell us exactly where this statement by Sergeant BRIGHT and the response by BEAN was made, as best as you can remember?
A: Sergeant BRIGHT was on the main trail.

Q: Where was BEAN?
A: I believe BEAN was standing on the smaller trail leading to the hooch.

Q: What happened next?
A: The next thing I remember was that BEAN was leading the woman into this – he took her and led her into this little field there.

Q: What do you mean when you say that he was leading her?
A: I believe he was taking her away from the group, that he grabbed her by the arm or something.

Q: Did you see BEAN take this woman away from the group?
A: Yes, sir, I was looking at the thing as a whole, I wasn't

paying that much attention to particulars. I know he got her away from the group, that is all I know.

Q: Your attention wasn't focused particularly on the woman and BEAN at that time, is that right?

A: When they went away from the group, no, sir, I guess not.

Q: Who was in this group?

A: Those Vietnamese women and children, I guess, sir.

Q: Would you describe as best as you can the age and sex of these people?

A: The woman was about maybe 30, maybe 25, maybe 35.

Q: Was this woman the one that BEAN led away?

A: Yes, sir.

Q: What about the other people?

A: There was some older girls there, and some rather small ones.

Q: What would you say was the age bracket of these people?

A: I couldn't be sure, sir. The smallest one was maybe three.

Q: And how many people were there in the group?

A: I'd say close to eight or nine, sir.

Q: What Marines were around the area of the children and the women.

A: I don't remember, sir.

Q: Were there Marines around?
A: Yes, I believe there were a couple of Marines there. Once they had the people outside the hooch, they set fire to it.

Q: How did you distinguish Lieutenant BEAN from any other person in there?
A: Well, I knew it was.

Q: Was there anyone else around when Sergeant BRIGHT and BEAN had the conversation about the kids?
A: I don't remember, sir.

Q: Were there other people there, Marines?
A: Yes, sir.

Q: Do you remember who any of those other people were?
A: The whole patrol was bunched up.

Q: Where, if any place, did BEAN take this woman?
A: He took her into the middle of this small field, sir.

Q: Up to this point, did you see any hostile movement by this woman?
A: No, sir, I didn't.

Q: At this point, did you see any hostile movement on the part of the women, or children?
A: No, sir.

Q: What happened with Lieutenant BEAN?

A: He just took the woman into the middle of the field and shot her, sir.

Q: Approximately, if you remember, how many times did he shoot her?

A: I'd say three to six times.

Q: Was it automatic fire?

A: Semi-automatic.

Q: Was there any obstruction by the way of trees, bushes, or otherwise between your position and Lieutenant BEAN?

A: No, sir.

Q: Did you see anyone else around that area?

A: I suppose I saw them, sir.

Q: What do you think you saw?

A: I guess a group of Vietnamese people.

Q: Did you see two Marines any place?

A: I believe there were a couple of Marines on the trail, the small trail leading to the hooch.

Q: Where were these Marines in relation to the point where the woman was taken from the group and taken to the field?

A: They would have been directly behind Lieutenant BEAN.

Q: Taking these two cups, and this can, I want you to position the woman, BEAN, and yourself, so we can see what your observation point of view was.

A: Yes, sir.

GC: Let the record reflect that the witness has taken the two cups and the can and placed them in approximately a 120 degree angle.

Q: Would you describe in as much detail as you can remember, how BEAN shot this woman?

A: I believe BEAN shoved the woman in front of him and had his rifle in one hand and was pushing the woman in front of him with the other. When they got to this spot where he shot her, I believe she started to turn around, sir. She moved her body like this (motioning to the right) and he shot her.

Q: When she turned around like that, did you see BEAN's hand on her?

A: Yes, sir, I believe he still had his hand on the back of her.

Q: What happened when – let me ask you this. Did you hear any shots fired?

A: Yes, sir.

Q: Did you see the shots fired?

A: The muzzle flash.

Q: Did you see the muzzle flash or any other indication?

A: I suppose I did, sir.

Q: What did the woman do?
A: She just dropped.

Q: Did she just drop straight down, or did she fall forward, or what?
A: Sort of forward, I guess.

Q: When she fell forward, did she put her arms out, or did she just go down?
A: I think she put her arms out, sir.

Q: Approximately how far would you say the muzzle was from this woman?
A: I'd say no more than one or two feet, sir.

Q: Did you think it was point blank-range?
A: Yes, sir.

Q: Did these shots continue as the woman fell?
A: Yes, sir.

Q: What kind of weapon was Lieutenant BEAN using?
A: It was an M-16.

Q: Are you sure of that?
A: Yes, sir.

Q: How was Lieutenant BEAN dressed at that time?
A: I suppose like everybody else.

Q: Do you remember what he had on?

A: If I told you, I would be assuming what he had on, sir.

Q: Did he have a helmet on?
A: I believe he did, sir.

Q: Did you see him with a helmet on?
A: I believe I did, sir.

Q: Did you see him with a helmet on?
A: I don't remember.

Q: Do you know whether or not he had a flak jacket?
A: I just assume he did.

Q: Did you have your flak jacket on?
A: Yes, sir.

Q: Was there anything unusual about his appearance?
A: Not that I can recall, sir.

Q: Did you recognize the face of the individual that shot the woman as being the face of Lieutenant BEAN, the man here today?
A: Yes, sir.

Q: After the shots were fired, did you see any movement from the area of the woman?
A: No, sir.

Q: Did you go over and examine the woman?
A: No, sir.

Q: Did you know whether anyone examined the woman?
A: No, sir, I don't think anyone did, sir.

Q: What did BEAN do?
A: I guess he just walked away, sir.

Q: Did you see him walk away?
A: Again, I suppose I did, but I don't recall.

Q: How would you describe the movement of this woman, or the action that took place on the part of this woman immediately before she was shot? Did she jerk around?
A: I don't believe so, sir, I just remember that she started to turn, I believe to her right side sort of like this (motioning to the right).

Q: Could you tell whether or not BEAN turned the woman with his hand?
A: No, sir, I couldn't tell.

Q: What next attracted your attention, what did you do next?
A: The next thing I remember is we were back on the trail, I believe we were going to move out, and somebody said – well, we could see the group of Vietnamese back by the hooch that was still burning. Somebody said that there were some women in there. I went back to check it out, as there might be some more children, then we returned to the patrol. Somebody burned something. The first time we came in there, I heard the remark that the kids didn't cry when their mother got killed, but

they do when they burn such-and-such. I don't know what the item was, sir.

Q: Do you remember who said that?
A: No, sir, I don't.

Q: Do you know who was in the vicinity that might have said that?
A: No, sir.

Q: Where did your patrol go from this hooch?
A: I guess we just returned to the LZ, sir.

Q: Did you follow BEAN's actions after he left the woman back at the area of the hooch?
A: No, sir.

Q: Do you know what BEAN did after he left the woman?
A: No, sir.

Q: Did he come to your group and make any remarks?
A: He came up to our group and asked me for a cigarette.

Q: Did he say anything else to you or your group at that time?
A: Not that I recall, sir.

Q: What was your position in your squad when you returned to the LZ?
A: I don't know, sir.

Q: As you went back to the camp did you see or hear BEAN make any remarks at that time?

A: I remember that I was talking to, I believe it was HILL and LUCIANO about what had happened. BEAN came up later and said something about if I had seen or said something about being tight with ADAMSEN, and that if I had seen a lot of my buddies blown away like he had that I would feel the same way about the Vietnamese. That was about all.

Q: You heard BEAN say this?

A: Yes, sir, he was talking to me, sir.

Q: Would you give your impression as nearly as you can remember of what he told you?

A: It was if I had seen more people, more of my friends killed, that I would feel the same way about the Vietnamese people.

Q: Same as whom?

A: I imagine the same as everybody else, sir.

Q: Did he say anything else in this particular conversation besides that?

A: He said that he and ADAMSEN were tight or something like that.

Q: Was ADAMSEN the man that was killed?

A: Yes, sir, Lieutenant BRIGHT's radio man.

Q: Was there anything else said that evening that you remember about what happened on that patrol?

A: No, sir.

Q: Did you hear anything about what happened on the other patrol?

A: Not that night, sir.

Q: When was the first time that you heard about it?

A: I heard about it from Lance Corporal STRONG, sir. It was after we had gotten back to the battalion area.

Q: And what did Lance Corporal STRONG have to say?

A: He said that – we were discussing whether or not it was the right thing to do, to go through the ville like that and kill the civilians without knowing for sure that they were Viet Cong.

Q: Knowing for sure, or not knowing for sure?

A: Not knowing for sure.

Q: Please continue.

A: It got around to where we discussed what happened. I believe I asked him if there were any women and children killed, or any children in particular, in the patrol he was on, and he said that there were. He said they shot at a woman with a baby in her arms.

Q: Did he relate at that time any other things that happened on the other patrol?

A: He just said that he was security and was glad that

he – he was a machine gunner also, sir – he said he was glad that he didn't have anything to do with the actual shooting.

Q: Can you remember anything else that he told you?
A: Not really, sir.

Q: Did you have any conversation with anyone else in your platoon or the company?
A: Yes, sir, after I talked to the chaplain, he talked to the Major.

Q: Who talked to the Major?
A: The chaplain, sir. Captain GRAINGER sent Sergeant HAINES over to get me, and he asked me why the Major wanted to see me. He told me it was the right thing to go back out that night because there were signs of enemy trying to sneak up on the perimeter. He also told me that when I went to talk to the Major, to not colour anything up or anything, and after this –

Q: Wait a minute. Was anything said about the chain of command?
A: Pardon me?

Q: Were you told at that time not to violate the chain of command?
A: At first they thought that I had gone directly to the Major, sir.

Q: Please answer the question. Was anything said about the chain of command?

A: Yes, sir.

Q: What?

A: I can't remember exactly, but I think when they first came up there, when Sergeant HAINES first brought me to see the Captain, the Captain said something like, What's this you've been talking to the Major, or something like that, and I told him that I hadn't talked to the Major, which I hadn't at that time, but I had talked to the chaplain.

Q: Before I interrupted you, you started to tell us about some of the conversation. Will you please tell us about that?

A: I got back where the machine guns were set up, LUCIANO and I –

Q: Where is this now?

A: We were set up along the road, sir. I had been dismissed and had went back to where we were set up. I had been there for maybe, I don't know how long it was, but then Lieutenant BAIRD came up and told me to do what I thought was right, and I just explained to him that I had gone to see the chaplain.

Q: What did you tell Lieutenant BAIRD?

A: In reference to my going to see the chaplain?

Q: Yes.

A: I can't remember, sir, I just said something about I can't see fighting that we don't know – I didn't understand that the situation should have been handled in that way. He couldn't either, and he said that he was a fine Christian man, or something like that.

Q: What did he say?

A: He said he was a Christian man.

Q: You are speaking now of Lieutenant BAIRD?

A: Yes, sir.

Q: Anything else?

A: He said that Sergeant BRIGHT was a fine man with a wife back in the States, but the other night he just took a man out and shot him.

Q: When was this conversation?

A: About two days or so after the operation.

Q: Do you remember any other parts of that conversation?

A: No, sir, that's about all he said. He said to do what I thought was right.

Q: I want you to back up and tell us as best you can remember, what you said, what the Lieutenant said, and how the conversation ran, would you do that for us, please?

A: He said, I want to talk to you, or something like that.

Q: Did he come up to you?

A: Yes, sir, he came over to our position.

Q: Who else was there at the time?

A: LUCIANO was, sir.

Q: Please continue.

A: We walked away from where LUCIANO was. He just came over and said, I guess I know how you feel, or something like this.

Q: Do you know any reason why he should come over and single you out?

A: Well, sir, he had been present when Captain GRAINGER was speaking to me, sir.

Q. Please continue.

A. I guess he just wanted me to know that I wasn't alone in the way I felt about what had happened. That's all I can tell you, sir.

Q. Please continue with the conversation you were having.

A. I just remember stating that I thought it wasn't right or something and he said, Neither can I. I can't see it either, or something like that. Then he said, I'm a Christian, he said, Now, Sergeant BRIGHT is a fine man. He's got a wife back in the States, but the other night he just took a man out and shot him. He said – I don't know if he said this in this conversation or in another conversation – but he said, If anybody thinks you're lying, I'll back you up.

Q: Do you know whether or not LUCIANO heard this conversation?

A: No, sir, he didn't.

Q: Did you have any other conversations?

A: Not that I recall, sir.

Q: How soon after you came back to the battalion area did you report this or did you talk to the chaplain?

A: I talked to the chaplain the day before the county fair.

Q: And when was the county fair in relation to the 22nd of October?

A: A couple of days after. I remember it was a couple of days. The county fair must have been about five or six days later, because I know that it was immediately after Operation Liberty II.

Q: Did you hear BEAN say anything else about what happened?

A: No, sir, I didn't.

Q: Did he say anything about the investigation or the rap, or the charges?

A: Nothing very important, sir. I remember talking to him a couple of times afterwards, this was after they had started the investigation back at the battalion.

Q: Do you remember anything he said?

A: I remember him telling me that he hadn't killed anybody. Later, after this investigation, I saw him go into

this Vietnamese laundry and he told me that he heard
that I was going back to Bravo company and I said,
Right, and he said, If you have anything to do with it,
I'm going to jail.

Q: Could you emphasize that any more?
A: That was about all I talked to him about, sir.

Q: Can you think of anything else to add that might be
helpful to us, or are you aware of any other facts that
happened on the night or early morning of 22 October?
A: I can remember that when we first went out on patrol
I could hear some shots, some screams, and then some
more shots, from the other patrol, I imagine.

Q: Did the screams come from the same area as the shots?
A: Yes, sir.

Q: I know it is very difficult, but can you distinguish, was
there a big volley of fire and then screams?
A: I can't say.

Q: You don't know.
A: Right.

Q: Can you think of anything else?
A: No, sir.

GC: We have no further questions, sir.

¶My first thought was that I'd missed it somehow: That if
I read the transcript again, and more carefully this time,
it would be there. Hidden somewhere in the text. But no
matter how many times I read the transcript through,
Owen appeared only as the nearly anonymous Carey.
Injured, and evacuated early on from the story, as though
he had been only a peripheral character, of no great significance to the account.

How was I to understand this?

Or in any way now recount the real events of that night,
the twenty-second of October, 1967? Or understand my
father's relationship to Owen? Or to Henry? Or, for that
matter, to my mother. Or Helen. Or me.

¶Several possibilities seem to present themselves.

1. That the events indeed occurred in the manner indicated by the transcript. That Owen had been injured and
removed from the squad. That he died later, in hospital,
as was indicated in the letter that was sent shortly after
his death, and which Henry still keeps in a drawer. That
the stories of my father, told to me in the summer before
his death, muddled by morphine and beer, were only
phantom images, resurfacing as in a dream, in shifting and
often contradictory arrangements of circumstance and
form.

2. That my father was not mistaken. That the events of the
twenty-second of October, 1967, played themselves out
more or less in the way that my father recounted to me.
That Owen had not been injured, and had accompanied

my father and Bean on patrol. That he had held up his hand
as if to stop a bullet that did not stop; that my father had
covered his body with his own. That it was only later that
these events were retracted, eliminating themselves from
the records. By Bean, perhaps, who in the laundry one day
had whispered a warning that was not fully accounted for
with the, "If you have anything to do with it ..." which,
in his testimony, my father recalled. Or, maybe it had even
been the watery-eyed Michael Baird who inspired my
father to the requisite caution; couching any offence in his
words by adding, for the record, "Do what you think is
right."

3. That the puzzling circumstances surrounding Bright
– that fine man, with the wife in the States – who took
a man out one night and shot him, are of some greater
importance to the story.

My father, questioned on this point still further in the
cross-examination, was unable to give the counsel any
further clues as to the identity of the man who was killed,
or the reason for such an indiscretion – if that's indeed
what it had been. I suppose that it was assumed that the
man had been a Vietnamese, suspected of Viet Cong ties,
but no indication is given to this, or any other, effect.

"Do you know," the cross-examiner had inquired of my
father, "that at the time of the twenty-second of October,
1967, Lieutenant Baird had known Sergeant Bright for only
about three days?"

"No, sir," my father, to this question, replied.

"Now this concern for Sergeant Bright's welfare is
touching," continued the cross-examiner. "And when he

told you that Sergeant Bright took a man out and shot him, did he tell you *he saw* Sergeant Bright take a man out and shoot him?"

"I don't think he said *I saw*, I think he said, just that Sergeant Bright *did it*."

"Did you ask for any verification?"

"No, sir."

"You just assumed that it was true."

"I guess I assumed it as being true, sir."

"You took his word for it."

"Yes, sir."

"Did you bother to ask him where he was when this happened?"

"No, sir, I didn't."

"Didn't it seem a little odd to you that this man, Lieutenant Baird, was coming to you and telling you on one hand, *Do what you think is right*, and on the other hand he was suggesting to you what *he* thinks is right? In other words, it is too bad, but after all they did kill people – did this strike you as being a little odd?"

"Yes, sir, it did. If he really felt it was wrong, why didn't he do something about it?"

"Would you think it a little more odd if I told you that he testified here today that he had never even talked to you?"

"What, sir?"

"He testified here today that he never talked to you concerning Sergeant Bright or anyone else."

"I'd have to say that is not the truth, sir."

¶According to Parada, there had been no further

interrogation into that particular event, and, after my father was asked to testify as to the moral character of Bright: "I thought he was a pretty good officer," my father said, the issue seems to have been dropped entirely, and to such a depth that even my father did not mention it again; not even when he said to me, "I've never told this to anyone," and spoke for the first time about the war.

I couldn't help but wonder if the man who disappeared that night – that Baird may or may not have seen killed – was my father's friend, and Henry's son. That whatever events had transpired (unrecorded by my father's version of things, said or unsaid, or by the transcript itself) had caused a second conflict to erupt that night. That my father should later have remembered it differently (imagining that he himself had witnessed the event of the death – that he was, in fact, through his own action, or lack thereof, *responsible* for that death) could be understood as a trick of the memory. It could even be understood as a not-wholly-unimaginable desire to obscure the exact nature of the death itself; its equivalent helplessness. Perhaps my father had hoped to create for himself, in the retelling at least, the idea that things might have come out differently in the end. That he himself might have had some power over what did, and did not happen on that particular night. Securing for himself, that is, in the recollection of an *actual moment*, an object to which he could attach the immensity and permanence of his guilt, and his loss – just as, for Frank Higgins, that loss had been expressed by the precise figure of three hundred men.

But I do not pretend to understand these events, or the holes in the stories, or the implications of what was said and unsaid in the two times (first at the trial, and second to me, shortly before his death) that my father spoke of his experiences on Operation Liberty II, and throughout the rest of the war. When I questioned Parada about the incongruencies between my father's stories and the documents to which I was later able to compare them to, he had little to offer by way of explanation. And though he did not seem to infer that my father had misconstrued, either mistakenly or otherwise, the nature of Owen's death, it was clear that he was no longer terribly concerned with the details of the thing, and that, having exhausted the resources with which he had planned to uncover the truth, it was as good as if the event had never occurred.

¶But I think differently. I think that the emphasis has been, through the wrong-way-round field glasses of time, reversed somehow. And that the actions that did or did not take place that night are somewhat sideways to the real story – just as the events of my father's life have been, I believe, somewhat sideways to himself. To the true story, that is, of his life: the one that I would have liked to have written. Because this, neither, is the real story. Still, the details get in, and still, everything is left out.

I believe, for example, that for my father and for the rest of my family, what remains now of this particular story is not the story itself, but something underneath. Because, even at the very end, there remained in my father's life, and now in my own, that possibility, always. A promise of something. And although now that promise – which I have been trying for some time now to put into words – happens to be at this moment trundling its way along

Highway 70, somewhere East of Columbus, on its way to Fargo, North Dakota, only just now disappearing from the limit of the story, it will continue to remain. Underneath everything. Etched in our minds. And not in its rough and unfinished form, either. As it existed in Roddy Stewart's, or my grandmother's, or Henry's garage. But as a real and honest-to-goodness boat, sailing up the coast of Maine from Booth Bay Harbor, Past Halifax and Chedabucto Bay. All the way to St. John's.

REMEMBER ME

Keith Douglas

Remember me when I am dead
and simplify me when I'm dead.

As the process of earth
strip off the colour and skin:
take the brown hair and blue eye

and leave me simpler than at birth,
when hairless I came howling in
as the moon entered the cold sky.

Of my skeleton perhaps,
so stripped, a learned man will say
"He was of such a type and intelligence," no more.

Thus when in a year collapse
particular memories, you may
deduce, from the long pain I bore

the opinions I held, who was my foe
and what I left, even in my appearance,
but incidents will be no guide.

Time's wrong-way telescope will show
a minute man ten years hence
and by distance simplified.

Through the lens see if I seem
substance of nothing: of the world
deserving mention or charitable oblivion,

not by momentary spleen
or love into decision hurled,
leisurely arrive at an opinion.

Remember me when I am dead
and simplify me when I'm dead.

ACKNOWLEDGEMENTS

I gratefully acknowledge the support of the citizens of Canada
and Nova Scotia, through the Canada Council for the Arts and
the Nova Scotia Department of Tourism, Culture and Heritage,
for their financial assistance during the completion of this
book. Many thanks are extended to Moez Surani, Mikhail Iossel,
Stephanie Bolster and Gary Blackwood for their help with this
manuscript at its various stages, as well as to Kate Kennedy,
Andrew Steeves and Gary Dunfield at Gaspereau Press for their
belief in this novel, and the vision and hard work that went into
its original publication in 2009. Thanks also to Jason Arthur at
William Heinemann for his keen editorial eye, and to my agent,
Tracy Bohan, for all of her encouragement and support. Finally, I
would like to thank my father, Olaf Skibsrud (1946–2008), who
shared with me his experiences upon which parts of this novel
are based, and whose "warmest heart" is – I hope – one of the
true subjects of this story.

The lines from "I sing of Olaf glad and big". Copyright © 1931,
1959, 1991 by the Trustees for the E.E. Cummings Trust. From
E.E. Cummings' *Complete Poems: 1904–1962*, edited by George J.
Firmage. Copyright © 1979 by George James Firmage. Used by
permission of Liveright Publishing Corporation. ¶ The William
James quotation is taken from Chapter V of *Pragmatism* (1907). ¶
The excerpt from no. 114 of John Berryman's *The Dream Songs* is
copyright © 1969 by John Berryman; copyright renewed in 1997
by Kate Donahue Berryman. Reprinted by permission of Farrar,
Straus and Giroux, LLC. ¶ The Gary Lane quotation is from *I Am:
A Study of E.E. Cummings' Poems*, published by the University Press of
Kansas; copyright © 1976. The complete text of Keith Douglas'
"Remember Me When I am Dead" is reproduced by permission
of Faber and Faber Ltd. ¶ I would also like to acknowledge
the use of material from the 1942 film production, *Casablanca*,
directed by Michael Curtiz and starring Humphrey Bogart,
Ingrid Bergman and Paul Henreid. ¶ Although all the names and
some of the details have been changed, the transcript included
in the epilogue is based on a real document produced during
the Article 32 investigation of the incident at Quang Tri, South
Vietnam, on 22 October 1967.

A NOTE ON THE TYPE

In 1928, the British sculptor, wood engraver and type designer
Eric Gill (1882–1940) moved to Pigotts in Buckinghamshire and
set up a workshop. Among his ventures there was the establish-
ment, in 1930, of a printing business with René Hague. As he
had done for the Golden Cockerel Press the previous year, Gill
designed a proprietary typeface for use at his press, naming it
after his daughter Joanna – who later married Hague. The H.W.
Caslon foundry cut punches for the roman in 1930, in time for
its use in the production of Gill's *An Essay on Typography*, which
appeared in June 1931, one of the first books produced by Hague
& Gill. A second edition, published by Sheed & Ward in 1936,
introduced Joanna's italic. In 1937, the Monotype Corporation
released a version of Joanna for their composition casters. A
digital version appeared in 1986, with semi-bold and bold
weights added by the Monotype drawing office.

Typeset by Andrew Steeves at Gaspereau Press, Kentville, Nova Scotia, Canada.

Read on to enjoy the wonderful short story
'Electric Man' from Johanna Skibsrud's
masterfully crafted story collection,
This Will Be Difficult to Explain
and Other Stories.

For Rebecca

THE FIRST TIME I saw him he was sitting out on the deck of the Auberge DesJardins, drinking something out of a tall glass. He had a broad-brimmed straw hat on, the kind that women wear, and he was reading *The Herald Tribune*. I was always looking out for *The Herald Tribune* that summer, because it indicated to me the English-speaking visitors when they came. Though I could no longer excuse the great loneliness of that summer by the dearth of English newspapers in the place, I was always happy to see *The Herald Tribune*.

The Auberge was a spot more popular among the Continentals. The Americans and the Brits and even most of the Australians stayed at the bigger resorts, closer to town. We kept mostly Swiss and Belgian visitors, many of whom had been coming to stay at the Auberge for many years, and so were not—as the Americans always seemed to be doing—simply passing through.

By that point in the summer, my French was good enough for just about every purpose except being able to actually *say* anything. My accent was all right, the guests all said so: I could carry it off. It wasn't marvellous, they didn't say that, but they did say, to my credit, that I didn't sound like an American, pretending, or—and this was worse—a Canadian, being sincere.

When I saw him the first time I was doing the afternoon rounds on the deck—sweeping through, as I did every four o'clock—collecting empty glasses and trays and asking if the guests were quite as comfortable as could be expected. Everyone mostly said that they were. The Auberge—especially out on the deck, in the pre-dinner hours—was a comfortable place, and very few people thought to complain. Except, of course, on the occasion that they should need a drink, or the bill, or else another drink, and then they did ask, but so politely—in so light and detached a way—that it was as if they wished to indicate that the lack, indicated by the request, was in fact just another element from which was composed an all-around satisfactory whole. One or two guests, however, over the course of the weeks that I stayed on at the Auberge, could be counted on to be more exacting than most. The man with the hat was, it turned out, one of those.

THE FIRST TIME I saw him was not the first time he saw me, and when I made my way over to his table and said, "Tout va bien, Monsieur?" because he looked like a man who didn't need a thing in the world, he said, "Non." He said: "I saw you pass this way fifteen minutes ago, and I tried to get your attention. There's not enough ice in my drink." He rattled his tall glass so that I could see that it was true.

From his accent I guessed he was from somewhere in the Northeast. Connecticut, New Hampshire, maybe, and I thought it was too bad that he could tell right away that I wasn't French. Usually it was just the people who really *were* French who could tell. But maybe, I thought, he was one of those guests whose French was so bad they didn't even try. Who just spoke English as though they expected everyone to understand, or else learn in a hurry.

"I'm sorry, sir," I said, in my friendliest voice. "We'll get that fixed up for you right away," and he said, "I didn't expect you to be from the South. I would have pegged you as being from Minnesota or something. St. Paul. Aren't you a little serious," he said, "for the South?"

I didn't know what he meant, but I knew he didn't mean to be nice. He had a teasing, half-mean look in his eye and held his glass away from me when I leaned over to take it away. I could tell he was going to be a most scrupulous guest, and any hope that I'd had for striking up more than the usual conversation with him was gone. I just wanted to get back to the kitchen, to get him more ice for his drink like he'd asked.

The glass itself, however, the man with the hat had by then retracted—just enough that I would have had to really reach for it in order to take it away. He watched me carefully as he held it there, at that particular distance, looking interested in what I might do. I didn't do anything. I just stood there with my hand—not extended, but just open and waiting between us—until he got bored with the game and simply handed me the glass.

That's the way things went for some time. He didn't like me very much, and I didn't like him. Or else he liked me too much, and I didn't like him. I couldn't decide, and neither one pleased me.

I could never please him, either. I wasn't, perhaps, quite *authentic* enough for him. Whenever I answered his questions—about where I had come from and why— he always gave me a suspicious sideways look, as if he supposed I was lying and he and I both knew it but we weren't going to say anything about it—at least for a while.

He was the one who asked questions—I never volunteered information on my own. And he never believed what I told him. It gave me an uncomfortable feeling, because his questions were never particularly complicated, and I had never before had anyone doubt the answers I gave to questions as simple as those.

I SAW A LOT of the man with the hat after that. He stayed on at the Auberge for the final part of July and most of August. Unlike the other guests, he didn't go into town, or take weekend excursions to Provence or down along the Côte d'Azur. Like me, he stayed at the Auberge pretty much all of the time.

I would see him in the mornings in the dining room when I delivered curled-up butter to the tables, and then later I would see him down at the beach, sitting in one of the Auberge's folding chairs, his woman's hat on, when I went down to the shore to collect the beach furniture that had been abandoned by the other guests. In the late afternoons, I would always see him on the deck, before the dining room reopened—he was always very prompt at mealtimes—and I would laboriously refill his tall glass with ice that, it seemed, melted unnaturally fast in his hands.

One afternoon, I said to Marie-Thérèse, who was a niece of Madame and Monsieur Rondelle, the owners of the Auberge, and had worked in the dining room three summers in a row, "Il n'est jamais contente!" As I spoke, I tossed my hands in the air in order to emphasize my disdain for a man who could never be *contente* with a thing. I was always talking with my hands in those days—to make up, I suppose, for how I always suspected my words to fall so short of whatever it was I was trying to say. Marie-Thérèse just shrugged. She was a very easygoing girl, quite *contente* herself, almost all of the time. "Quelque personnes," she told me, "sont comme ça." She shrugged again, and went out onto the deck to check on a guest, who was just then at the very beginning stages of needing something.

The way she said it, "sont comme ça," as if it were the most inevitable and insignificant thing that it should be so, made me feel a little foolish for having allowed myself to be so bothered by the hatted man, who was—as Marie-Thérèse said a little later—obviously "un peu cuckoo." As she said it, she wound her finger as if around an invisible spool beside her ear, rolling her eyes up into her head so just the bottom bits of her irises showed.

IN THE EARLY AFTERNOONS, before I had to go up to the deck to refill the guests' drink with ice, and take away and refill the trays with little things to eat, I would always go down to the beach myself, and lie out on one of the long fold-out chairs, in the shade. I always covered myself up completely, even in the shade, on account of my fair skin, which was so easily burned. I wasn't like the French girls who just got browner and browner as the summer wore on and could lie out from ten to two o'clock and not get burned, even on their most sensitive spots, which were also bare.

Because everyone else preferred the sun, I had my shady spots all to myself, and the beach felt secluded and private in the places that I chose. I liked it that way. It was a change from the constant hum of the Auberge, which was busy in the high season. Also, it made me feel as though, at least in those moments, I had control over my solitude. That it was a thing I had chosen.

Sometimes I would try to read, but I was allowing myself to read only French books during the day, and that was difficult. I could never get into the plot of anything. I understood the words, that wasn't the problem—it was just that that was all they seemed to be to me on the page. Just little, individual words—each one isolate, and independent of any of the other little words, which I also understood, and therefore not seeming to be continuous, in any broader sense, beyond their exact and independent meaning.

So after a little reading I would give up, and put the book down on the sand, and stare around at the beach and out to the water, which always looked very blue and warm, even though if I ever went down to it, it turned out to be cold. Also, it was green and brown up close, and not brilliant and blue as it had looked from afar.

For some time I was always re-convinced from a distance that the next time I went down to the water it would really be how it appeared. But after a while I stopped going down at all. I didn't like to keep finding that I'd—again—been wrong.

So I stayed up in the shady spot that I had all to myself instead, not reading, and just looking around. I had redis-covered an old habit of mine, which was to look at things through a narrowed field of vision by cupping my hand around my eye. In this way I would reduce the world to such a small point—my palm curled like a telescope, and one eye closed—that all I could see was one particular thing. For example, I would look out at the ocean and narrow my palm in that way so that all I could see, beyond my own hand, was a completely uniform shade of blue, uninterrupted by any other shade, or by any of the noise and commotion of the bathers, who stayed in the shallow parts, near shore. Or else I would turn my head and with my telescope eye see just the top bit of a sail. Or a radar reflector—glinting in the sun. Seeing neither, that is, the radar or the sun, but instead just—that *glinting*; just the reflection of metal and light.

It was, indeed, an old habit—back from when I was a kid, and would go out into the small front yard of my mother's house in Jacksonville and look at things like that, just a little at a time. After a while I knew the whole front yard that way—in small sections, each the size of a dime. What I liked best was to look at the natural things: the grass and the little scrubby flowering bushes in my mother's garden by the porch—and the sky. I could pretend that the rest of everything didn't exist. That I was a different sort of girl, who lived in the country instead of in town, and was surrounded by wilderness on all sides.

When I had chosen one unblemished spot, one particular, dime-sized part of the yard, I would concentrate on it very hard. I would try to press myself, every bit of myself, into that small space left between my palm and the curled-up pinky finger of my right hand. To rush right out of myself, just as—I imagined—that other girl, who was not me, and yet was ever so much more me than I myself could ever have been—might do.

It was a tingling, rushing, electric sensation that I felt coursing through my body then, when I tried so hard to push myself into the fragments of the lawn, and experience the world in the whole and real way that another (I imagined) might. Like maybe the little bits of me were on fire and if I didn't get pressed into the spot that I wanted to press myself into, I might burn up and be gone.

It seemed important. To be able to get into blades of grass the way that I wanted to. Or into the two or three spots in the sky that weren't marked up by tall houses, or telephone poles.

ONE AFTERNOON, down by the shore in front of the Auberge, just as I had set down my book that I wasn't really reading, the man with the hat came over and set up his chair next to mine. I saw him from a distance before he came. Before, that is, it was clear to me that it was in my direction, specifically, that he would come.

He was carrying his chair, and walked slowly, the chair banging on his leg with every second step. I made a tunnel of my right hand and held it up to my right eye, squinting the left so that it was entirely closed. Then I followed his hat, just the broad brim of his hat, until, when I took my hand away from my eye, I realized that he was almost upon me, and he could see very well what I was doing. I wiped my eyes, surprised, and then continued to do so as he approached, as if I hoped us both to believe that it was what I'd been doing all along. He put up his hand in greeting but didn't say anything until he had settled—quite near me—into his chair.

"Hello," he said, naturally. As if, outside of my working hours, he respected that I was in no way responsible for any discomfort of his.

229

"Hello," I said. But I was wary. I wondered what he would ask me, because he didn't have a drink, and I didn't have any ice.

"You probably don't know this about me," he said. "I'm a painter."

"Oh?" I asked, but he didn't say anything more. "That's interesting," I said. "What sort of painting do you do?"

"Landscapes mostly," he told me. Then paused again. "But I've been meaning"—he kept his eye on me as he spoke—"to try a portrait someday." Again he paused. "I was wondering," he said finally, "if you would be willing to sit for me someday soon."

Because I didn't have a proper reason to refuse, I said that I would, and the next evening, as we'd arranged, I knocked on the door of his third floor room. I could hear him shout from the inside that I should come in, so I did, and there he was, sitting in one of the straight-backed chairs that were provided in the more modest rooms. Next to him was a dish of watercolours and a small stretched canvas. He had been waiting for me. He didn't have an easel or anything, and his watercolours appeared unused. There was another straight-backed chair opposite him with an uneven table behind it. On the table was a small lamp that cast a limited light around the otherwise dim room. I had made—I thought suddenly—a rather large mistake. He wasn't a real painter, that was obvious now—and was perhaps even more *cuckoo*, as Marie-Thérèse had said, than we had originally supposed.

I thought it best if I left immediately. Quickly and discreetly. And in the future—I thought—be even more certain not to disturb, or trouble, the man with the hat. But instead of leaving, and for somewhat of the same reason that I agreed in the first place—because I could not think how to refuse—I sat down in the chair he had arranged for me, opposite his own.

"Let me guess," he said, after a while—he was sketching away at the canvas, with an ordinary pencil, his paints laid aside. Every now and then he would look up at me, but more often he looked down at the pencil. "Let me guess," he said. "You wanted to be an—actress when you were a girl."

It was not what I expected to hear. "No," I said. I never had wanted to be an actress. I supposed he'd said it imagining that all girls who agreed to sit for portraits imagined themselves that way, then or at some other, earlier time of their lives. That they were all aware, and wanted to be made more so, of their own particularness, their singularity.

I liked the movies, but the theatre seemed exaggerated to me. It always rang a little false. One time I'd gone up north to a festival in Savannah with my friend Ariane. We sat right up front for a production of A Single Afternoon, which was put on by a British company that Ariane had told me I'd enjoy. They were "naturalists"—like in the movies. "They even have the backstage set up to look like another room of the set," she explained. "So the actors don't get out of character between scenes."

I had never been more bored in my life. Even Ariane was bored. You could feel it—boredom everywhere. Soon even the actors started to feel it. They sped up their lines, and started to look angry, when it didn't seem "right" or "real" that they should.

Not even midway through, Ariane leaned over and said, "I'm depressed."

We were sitting so close to the stage that at a certain point—surely things were now drawing to a close—one of the actors came forward, so close that I could have reached up and touched him—and I did. Without really thinking—I did. I reached out and touched his foot, which was clothed in a very ordinary sock—the thick, pilly wool kind that lots of men wear, and that on occasion I had even worn myself.

Ariane, even with how into "making a scene" she was in those days, was horrified, and leaned away from me, as if in reflex. She looked at me from that new distance as though she had never seen me before in her life. It was no ordinary boundary, the look suggested, that I had crossed. The actor himself gave a kind of a jump when I touched him, and then shot me a startled and irritated glare. We were so close that I could see every line, and every slight change in the expression, on his face. He was older than he was pretending to be.

It was just: there was something ridiculous and sad about those socks. I wanted to touch them. All of a sudden, seeing them so close, all the little pilly hairs shooting off from them in all directions, I'd thought, isn't it the saddest thing in the world that there was this sock—what seemed to me the single realest sock I'd ever seen—up there, in front of me on the stage, and it was pretending *not* to be a sock, or at least to be a sock in *another* afternoon, a sock that it, so evidently, was not.

A sock that would be realer than the sock that it *actually was*, was a thing that I could not imagine.

I TOLD THE MAN with the hat that I hadn't ever wanted to be an actor. The closest I had come, I said, when he seemed surprised, was in a fourth-grade play when I was supposed to play a crow. "I didn't have any lines," I told the man. "I was just supposed to fly around in the background, but that was fine by me."

"I imagine you were a very good crow," the man said with a little smile. He had picked up his tray of paints and was beginning to dab at the canvas.

"I wasn't," I said. "I called in sick. My mother dressed me in the costume and painted my face, but then I looked in the mirror and started to cry. Nothing my mother could do could get me to leave the house looking like that."

"I guess I was wrong," the man said.

"I just kept saying," I told him, "'I don't want to be a crow! You can't make me!'" I laughed, but the man—who was not wearing his hat on this occasion—did not.

"That's sad," he said. His old sideways look was back. It seemed his remark may have even been a sort of reproach.

For laughing at something that he saw—and that I should see too—wasn't very funny at all.

Well, it was *my* story.

"Oh, it's okay," I said. I didn't think it was sad. "I thought I was supposed to be too *serious* anyway."

I WENT BACK TWO OR three more times to sit for the guest. In the daytime, we resumed our old routines, and he never mentioned anything about the painting when he saw me. Strangely, he didn't try to talk to me, either, as he had done before when I refilled his drink with ice in the late afternoons. He seemed more distant, and formal, as if we had never met at all, and that made me feel a little strange about the whole thing—as though I'd had a love affair with the old man, instead of simply sitting in a chair.

We acted like that with each other, for some reason. Overly polite and conventional like that. We didn't, either of us—as is often the case with the more humid matters of the heart—know quite how to understand the breach (though it had been, in our case, only the smallest, almost undetectable, tear) of our independence from one another, which we otherwise would have maintained.

ONE DAY, WHILE HE WAS working away without even looking up at my face, which often for long stretches he was able to do, I said, "Why did you think that? Why did you ask me that before—if I'd wanted to be an actress?"

He said only, as I had suspected: "Doesn't every young girl?" And shrugged. He did not seem in the mood to discuss anything.

But instead of letting the subject drop, as I might have, I said I didn't think all young girls *did* want to be actresses. I said it was an unfair thing to assume. I guess that I was feeling a little hurt, because I'd thought, if nothing else, that he was a man who paid attention to things. Who was perceptive, and had perhaps seen something in me, something particular, that had made him ask that question, instead of its springing from either mere supposition or form.

So maybe I liked, after all, the way that he looked at me sideways when I answered his questions, as if I thought for a moment, too, with that look, that I had made it all up—that the details of my life weren't really my own. That I was perhaps someone altogether different—whose particulars I didn't, or was just about to, know.

But later he said, "I myself was an actor, you know," and I said, "I thought you were a painter," and he said, "A person can be more than one thing."

"Okay," I said. "So what kind of actor were you?" He could be amusing after all.

"You just struck me," he said, in answer to my previous question, and ignoring the last, "like me in a way. Like someone"—he looked up for the first time in a while—"who wishes they were more than they are in real life, or at least something—somebody—else sometimes. That's an acting technique," he told me. "I suppose you wouldn't know that. Starting from zero so that then you can become something, or someone, entirely new." He was working away diligently with the paints, the small canvas tilted—always—up and away from me so that I couldn't see the progress that he made. "That's what you should have done when you were a crow," he told me. "Your problem was seeing yourself as a little girl who *looked* like a crow, and not being the crow yourself." I nodded, and made a small sound like I was interested, and understood. He didn't seem embarrassed at all to say what he had, and I did think *that* was interesting. What he said really did strike me as an essentially embarrassing thing to say. *To admit*, that is, that you were not, in and of yourself, *enough*. And would remain that way. To my American sense of things, which I—and I assumed that he, too—had retained (he had the accent, after all, stronger than my own), well, wasn't that the very worst thing that a person could admit?

"I don't think that's me," I told him quickly. "I think I'm all set to be just me. Just as I am."

"So I was wrong again," the man said, shrugging his shoulders again, like it was no big deal. "Just with me, it's different," he said after a while, "because I really was an actor."

"Right," I said. "What kind of actor did you say that you were?"

"A circus performer," the man said. "I was the Electric Man in the Bulgarian Circus."

I laughed even though he didn't. "The electric man?" I said. I tried to become serious again, as if I had been all along. "What's that?"

"Oh," he said, putting his paints aside. "Oh, you don't know about that, either." And then he told me about how it was to be an Electric Man in the Bulgarian Circus. How every night he would go out into the ring, and put his hands on a shiny metal ball, and be pumped through with electricity that the silver ball shot out so that his hair stood up on his head and his clothes got singed and sometimes at the end of the night he would have small wounds on the tips of his fingers where the electricity had had nowhere else to go in his body and so burned its way out. "The crowd loved me the best," the man said. He never wore his hat in the room, and he was bald as an apple. "I never saw it myself, from my position, but they said that from the stands I *glowed*."

"That's just crazy," I said, but I was impressed. I didn't know, of course, if I should believe him or not, but then I didn't see why not, or what purpose it would serve either of us if I didn't. "Did it hurt?" I asked. I remembered sticking my fingers into the electrical outlets at home sometimes, when I was a little kid. How much *that* had hurt. I did it more than once, but maybe no more than three times. You'd think it wouldn't have taken more than the once, but I just always wondered at what point the electricity would arrive out of those tiny little slots where it looked like nothing could be.

"Oh yes," the Electric Man told me, busying himself again with the task of my portrait. "Oh yes, it hurt very much," he said. He picked up his tray of paints again and gazed down at the small canvas. It appeared that he did not want to talk after that, and after a quarter of an hour went by in which we didn't speak at all, I asked him if he thought one day soon I could see the portrait. He said, "I leave tomorrow, you can see it then." And then a little while later, he got up and said: "That will do."

IN THE MORNING HE was not downstairs when I did the rounds with the butter, and when I went about by the shore collecting chairs and parasols from the beach I did not see him there either—shielded, as usual, by the broad rim of his woman's straw hat.

He must have slipped out while I was down by the shore, because when I returned to the Auberge there was no one whose ice melted so fast and I spent the lazy pre-dinner hours casually refilling trays for the few guests who ate their little things very slowly and never seemed to need anything.

As usual, just before dinner, I checked my mail slot in the lobby of the Auberge, though there was rarely anything to find, and there it was: the small canvas, all wrapped up inside a rather tattered paper bag. I felt relieved—and not a little flattered. All that time, it would seem now, the painting had been just for me. But when I tore away the wrapping I saw that what he had left me was not a portrait at all, but the most banal seascape, not unlike the one outside the window of the Auberge, which the man with the hat would have seen quite clearly over my shoulder as I sat for all those hours opposite him in a straight-backed chair.

For a moment, I still hoped that he had kept the real portrait of me for himself and had given me this canvas only as a sort of substitute. But then I thought that it wasn't very likely: I had only ever seen one canvas in the little room. It seemed the man was, after all, perhaps quite literally, insane. I felt disappointed, and was about to make my way back to my room, when I noticed there was something else in the bag. It was the broad-brimmed hat, all rolled up—I hadn't imagined it could be made so small. It had a note attached to it, too, which said, in childish scrawl, *Because you're fair, like me, and must burn easily in too much sun.*

WHEN, A DAY OR TWO after that, I returned a stack of French novels to the little library that the owners kept in the Auberge's lounge, I slipped the canvas in with the books because I didn't want to look at it anymore. There was something very sad to me about the uniform blue of the ocean and the perfect little *m*'s for birds that had been drawn onto the sky. I wanted to get rid of it, but I didn't want to just throw it away.

My routine continued, unchanged by the Electric Man's absence. I made my rounds with the butter in the morning, and then went down to the beach, where I collected abandoned chairs and parasols, and then stretched out in the shade—covered head to toe so I wouldn't burn, and wearing the Electric Man's broad-brimmed hat. I still did that—still stretched out on the beach in the shade—even after I'd stopped going down to the water anymore because it was actually cold and green, or pretending to read French novels because none of the words ever seemed to hang together in a consecutive way.

I would just stare around, my hand curled to my eye sometimes, like a telescope. A strange sort—most basic sort—of telescope, of course; it never made anything appear any closer, or farther away. I never tried to summon myself, as I had done as a child. Never tried to press myself—myself as I *felt myself to be*, most truly—through the small space that was left between my farthest-away finger and the curve of my thumb. I think I didn't want to risk finding that, were I to try, I wouldn't feel that tingling, rushing electric sensation that I had when I was a child.

Someday, I thought, while I lay stretched out on an Auberge chair in the shady spot of the beach—before returning to refill the trays and pass out drinks and bills, and then drinks again, to the late-afternoon guests—I would try it again. I would try to feel myself *alive* again in the way that I had when I was very young. Perhaps the Electric Man had inspired me. To find that "blank space" of myself—or whatever it was he had said. There was no real *reason*, after all, I thought to myself, that I could not feel that way again—it was, in fact, quite possible, and someday, I thought, when I was feeling particularly well, I would try.

THEN, AT THE VERY END of August, perhaps a week or two after I had last seen the Electric Man, Madame Rondelle, the owner of the Auberge, stopped me on the stair. "I had a note from Monsieur Wyatt," she said. She always spoke to me in English, because she was no more French than me, though she spoke the language more perfectly. She was a Swede, but of course her English, as well as her French, was impeccable. I rarely saw her long enough to speak with her, though, and, in addition, she always made me nervous. She seemed so sure of herself all the time, and because I was never sure of anything, especially that summer, I always suspected that I was misunderstanding things—even in my own language. I had got that used to second-guessing.

I didn't even know who Monsieur Wyatt was, for example.

"Who?" I asked.

Madame Rondelle looked up at me, sharply. "The man with the hat," she told me. "He knows *you*," she said. "He said to give you a kind hello." She hesitated then, before stepping away—evidently wanting to say something more, but for some reason uncertain. "A very *dear* man," she told me, as if that were an explanation of something. "I'm a friend of his sister. He's been coming here for years." Then she hesitated again. "A little strange," she said, and her hand left the railing where she had placed it and fluttered up to her chest, as if it hoped to retain something there. "But a very *dear* dear man," she insisted, as if that settled it. But still she did not immediately move to go, and in the space of time in which we both lingered—she on the stair, about to decide whether to finally complete her ascent, and I at the bottom, equally unsure of whether I should relieve her of the conversation, make some excuse to go—I tried to think of some perfect thing to say to her of him. But I couldn't think of anything. I didn't want to tell her about the painting, that was certain. Someday she would find it, in going through the library, and throw it out; I didn't think she should know anything of its history if that were to be the case.

"What does he do now?" I asked, for want of anything else. "I mean," I said, "how is it he has the time, and the—" I paused, "the resources, I mean, to stay?" Then I realized I'd been rude. But I wanted to know. I didn't imagine that a former member of the Bulgarian Circus would have a very large pension. I presumed, in that moment, because I had never thought of it before, that he must have been from one of those large and wealthy New England families who could afford to finance, and be responsible for, the whims—however fleeting—of their members. It was because that suddenly seemed clear to me that I thought with some shame that it would have been better for me not to have mentioned the money at all. Money was embarrassing when there was either too much or too little of it, and the means to the Electric Man's situation—which was evidently comfortable—would have been better left unspoken.

But Madame did not seem perturbed by the question. If anything she adopted a more conciliatory tone. "From what I gather," she said—she began her ascent once more as she spoke, but slowly—"he gets a fairly sizeable cheque from Veterans of Foreign Wars." It would have been difficult to say whether she had whispered or shouted the words. There seemed, anyway, to be equal attention paid to both emphasizing and concealing the information that the sentence contained. Then she shrugged. "That's what gets forwarded here," she said.

I must have looked surprised, or like I was about to say something, and I don't think that she wanted to be detained much longer. "He got wounded badly in one of the wars," she explained—as if she wished now that she hadn't brought it up at all. "I'm not sure which one, he was in so many. Sam—that's his sister, my friend—she believes"—she had almost reached the top of the stair; pretty soon she would disappear—"they pay him to keep quiet about certain things, you know, that are too—" she paused again, just slightly, just before she was lost to the upstairs of the Auberge and said, "too awful to talk about." She had another tone in her voice now, a very sad faraway note had crept in, and her hand had remained at her throat as she mounted the stair. "He used to bathe down at the shore when he first came with Sam," she said. "But for some reason, he's stopped bathing now." She looked down to where I stood—it seemed a great distance. "It used to give me quite a fright to see him," she continued. Then she made a face, and tossed her hand that had been held at her throat in the air as if whatever she'd wished to hold as she'd ascended was useless to her now. "Just—awful," she said, "his whole body all scarred over the way it was. Whatever it was that happened to him, I don't know. But I should *hope*," she said, "that he's getting, for it, a pretty compensation." With a slight nod then, which served to mark her final departure, she turned, and continued up the stairs.